A HERITAGE OF STARS

There is no question that at one time, perhaps five hundred years ago, Earth was possessed of an intricate and technological civilisation. Of this, nothing operational remains. The machines and the technology were destroyed, perhaps in a few months' time. And not only that, but, at least at this university, and we suppose otherwhere as well, all or most of the literary mention of the technology also was destroyed. Here, certainly, all the technological texts are gone and in many instances allusions to technology contained in other books, not technological in nature, have been edited by the ripping out of pages . . .

From all indications that we have at this date, the collapse of civilisation came about because of an outrage on the part of what must have been a substantial portion of the populace against the kind of world that technology had created, although the outrage, in many instances, may have been misdirected . . .

Clifford D. Simak

A Heritage
of Stars

MAGNUM BOOKS
Methuen Paperbacks Ltd

A Magnum Book

A HERITAGE OF STARS
ISBN 0 417 02840 7

First published in Great Britain 1978
by Sidgwick & Jackson Ltd
Magnum edition published 1979

Copyright © Clifford D. Simak 1977

Magnum Books are published by
Methuen Paperbacks Ltd
11 New Fetter Lane, London EC4P 4EE

Made and printed in Great Britain
by Richard Clay (The Chaucer Press) Ltd
Bungay, Suffolk

1

One of the curious customs to arise out of the Collapse was the practice of pyramiding robotic brain cases, in the same manner that certain ancient Asiatic barbarians raised pyramids of human heads that later turned to skulls, to commemorate a battle. While the brain-case custom is not universal, there is enough evidence from travelers' tales to show that it is practiced by many sedentary tribes. Nomadic peoples, as well, may have collections of brain cases, but these are not pyramided except on ceremonial occasions. Ordinarily they are stored in sacred chests which, when the band is on the march, are given positions of honor, carried in wagons at the head of the column.

Generally, it has been believed that this fascination with robotic brain cases may commemorate man's triumph over the machines. But there is no undeniable evidence that this is so. It is possible that the symmetry of the cases may have an esthetic appeal quite apart from any other real or imagined signifi-

Clifford D. Simak

cance. Or it may be that their preservation is an unconscious reaction to a symbolic permanence, for of all things created by technological man, they are the most durable, being constructed of a magic metal that defies both time and weather.

—From Wilson's *History of the End of Civilization*

2

Thomas Cushing hoed potatoes all the afternoon, in the small patch on the bench above the river, between the river and the wall. The patch was doing well. If some unforeseen disease did not fasten on it, if it were not raided on some dark night by one of the tribes across the river, if no other evil fell upon it, come harvest time it would yield up many bushels. He had worked hard to produce that final harvest. He had crept on hands and knees between the rows, knocking potato beetles off the vines with a small stick he held in one hand and catching them as they fell in the bark container he held in the other hand. Catching them so they would not crawl from where they fell into the vines again, to feast upon the leaves. Crawling up and down the rows on his hands and knees, with his muscles screaming at the punishment, with a pitiless sun hammering at him so that he seemed to creep in a miasmatic fog composed of dead and heated air mixed finely with the dust that his crawling raised. At intervals, when the bark container was nearly full of the squirming, confused and deprived bugs, he'd go down to the riverbank, first marking the spot where he had ceased his labor, with the stick planted in the soil; then, squatting on the bank, he'd reach far out to empty the container into the flowing stream, shaking it vigorously to dislodge the last of the beetles, launching them upon a journey that few of them would survive, and carrying those few that would survive far from his potato patch.

In his mind, at times, he had talked to them. I wish you no harm, he'd told them; I do this not out of malice but to protect myself and others of my kind, removing you so you'll not eat the food on which I and others count. Apologizing to them, explaining to them to take away their wrath as ancient, prehistoric hunters had apologized and explained ritually to the bears they had slaughtered for a feast.

In bed, before he went to sleep, he'd think on them again, seeing them once again, a striped golden scum caught in the swirl of water and carried rapidly away to a fate they could not understand, not knowing why or how they'd come to such a fate, powerless to prevent it, with no means of escaping it.

And having dumped them in the river, back to crawling between the rows once more to gather other bugs to consign to the selfsame fate.

Then, later in the summer, when days went by with no rain falling, with the sun striking down out of the cloudless blue bowl of the sky, carrying buckets of water from the river on a yoke slung across his shoulders to supply the thirsty plants the moisture that they lacked; day after day trudging from the river's edge up the sharp slope to the bench, lugging water for his crop, then going back again to get two more pails of water, on an endless treadmill so the plants would grow and thrive and there would be potatoes stored against the winter. Existence, he had thought, survival so hard and dearly bought—a continual fight to assure survival. Not like those ancient days Wilson had written about so long ago, reaching back with fumbling fingers to try to create the past that had come to an end centuries before he had put quill to paper, forced to exercise a niggling economy of paper—writing on both sides of each sheet, leaving no margins on either side of the page, with no whiteness left at either top or bottom. And always that small and niggardly, that painfully small, script, so that he could cram in all the words seething in his brain. Agonizing over the concern that he mentioned time and time again—that the history he wrote was based more on myth and legend than on fact, a situation that could not be avoided since so little fact remained. Yet, convinced it was paramount that the history be written before what little fact remained completely disappeared, before the myth and legend had become more distorted than they already were. Agonizing, as well, over his measurement of myth and legend, sweating over his evaluation of them; asking himself, time and time again, "What should I put in? What should I leave out?" For he did not put in all of it; some he had left out. The myth about the Place of Going to the Stars he had left out.

But enough of Wilson, Cushing told himself; he must get back to his hoeing and his weeding. Weeds and bugs were enemies. The lack of rain, an enemy. The too hot sun, an enemy. It was not only he who thought so: there were others working patches of corn and potatoes that lay on other tiny benches, so much like his own, all up and down the river, close enough to the walls to gain some protection against the occasional raiders from across the river.

He had hoed all the afternoon and now, with the sun finally gone behind the river bluffs looming to the west, he crouched beside the river and stared across the water. Upstream, a mile or so, stood the stone piers of a ruined bridge, with some of the

5

bridge's superstructure still remaining, but nothing one could use to cross the river. Still farther upstream, two great towers rose up, former living structures that the old books called high rises. There had been, it appeared, two such types of structures—ordinary high rises and high rises for the elderly—and he wondered briefly why there should have been such age distinction. No such thing was true today. There was no distinction between the young and old. They lived together and needed one another. The young provided strength and the old provided wisdom and they worked together for the benefit of all.

This he had seen when he first came to the university and had experienced himself when he had been taken in under the sponsorship of Monty and Nancy Montrose, the sponsorship in time becoming more than a formal sponsorship, for he had lived with them and had become, in effect, their son. The university and, most of all, Monty and Nancy, had given him equality and kindness. He had, in the last five years, become as truly a part of the university as if he had been born to it and had known what he came to recognize as a unique kind of happiness that, in his years of wandering, he had not known elsewhere. Now, hunkering on the river's bank, he admitted to himself that it had become a nagging happiness, a happiness of guilt, chained here by the sense of affectionate loyalty to the aged couple who had taken him in and made him a part of them. He had gained much from his five years here: the ability to read and write; some acquaintance with the books that, rank on rank, lined the stacks of the library; a better understanding of what the world was all about, of what it once had been and what it was at the present moment. Given, too, within the security of the walls, the time to think, to work out what he wanted of himself. But though he'd worked at it, he still did not quite know what he wanted of or for himself.

He remembered, once again, that rainy day of early spring when he had sat at a desk in the library stacks. What he had been doing there he had now forgotten—perhaps simply sitting there while he read a book which presently he would replace upon the shelves. But he did recall with startling clarity how, in an idle moment, he had pulled out the desk drawer and there had found the small pile of notes written on flyleaves that had been torn from books, written in a small and crabbed hand, niggardly of space. He recalled that he had sat there, frozen in surprise, for there was no mistaking that cramped and economic writing. He had read the Wilson history time and time again, strangely fascinated by it, and there was no question in his mind, not the slightest question, that these were Wilson's notes, left here in the desk drawer to await discovery a millennium after they'd been written.

With trembling hands he had taken them from the drawer and laid them reverently on the desk top. Slowly he read through them in the waning light of the rainy afternoon and there was in them much material that he recognized, material that eventually had found its way into the history. But there was a page of notes—really a page and a half—that had not been used, a myth so outrageous that Wilson must finally have decided it should not be included, a myth of which Cushing had never heard and of which, he found upon cautious inquiry later, no one else had ever heard.

The notes told about a Place of Going to the Stars, located somewhere to the west, although there was no further clue to its location—simply "in the west." It all was horribly fuzzy and it sounded, in all truth, more like myth than fact—too outrageous to be fact. But ever since that rainy afternoon, the very outrageousness of it had haunted Cushing and would not let him be.

Across the wide turbulence of the river, the bluffs rose sheer above the water, topped by a heavy growth of trees. The river made sucking sounds as it rushed along, a hurrying tide that stormed along its path and, beneath the sucking sounds, a rumbling of power that swept all in its course. A powerful thing, the river, and somehow conscious and jealous of its power, reaching out and taking all that it could reach—a piece of driftwood, a leaf, a bevy of potato bugs, or a human being, if one could be caught up. Looking at it, Cushing shivered at its threat, although he was not one who should have felt its threat. He was as much at home in or on the river as he would be in the woods. This feeling of threat, he knew, was brought on only by a present weakness, born of vague indecision and not knowing.

Wilson, he thought—if it had not been for that page and a half of Wilson's notes, he'd be feeling none of this. Or would he? Was it only Wilson's note, or was it the urge to escape these walls, back to the untrammeled freedom of the woods?

He was, he told himself somewhat angrily, obsessed with Wilson. Ever since the day he had first read the history, the man had lodged himself inside his mind and was never far away.

How had it been with Wilson, he wondered, on that day of almost a thousand years ago, when he first had sat down to begin the history, haunted by what he knew would be its inadequacy? Had the leaves outside the window whispered in the wind? Had the candle guttered (for in his mind the writing always took place in candlelight)? Had there been an owl outside, hooting in derision at the task the man had set himself to do?

How had it been with Wilson, that night in the distant past?

3

I must write it clearly, Hiram Wilson told himself, so that in the years to come all who wish may read it. I must compose it clearly and I must inscribe it neatly, and most importantly, I must write it small, since I am short of paper.

I wish, he thought, that I had more to go on, that I had more actual fact, that the myth content were less, but I must console myself in the thought that historians in the past have also relied on myth, recognizing that although myth may be romanticized and woefully short of fact, it must, by definition, have some foundation in lost happenings.

The candle's flame flared in the gust of wind that came through the window. In a tree outside, a tiny fluffed-out screech owl made a chilling sound.

Wilson dipped the quill in ink and wrote, close to the top of the page, for he must conserve the paper:

*An Account of Those Disturbances Which Brought About
an End to the First Human Civilization (always
in the hope there will be a second, for
what we have now is no civilization,
but an anarchy)
Written by Hiram Wilson at the University of Minnesota
on the Banks of River Mississippi, This Account
Being Started the First Day of October, 2952*

He laid the quill aside and read what he had written. Dissatisfied, he added another line:

*Composed of Facts Gathered From Still Existing Books
Dating From Earlier Days, From Hearsay Evidence
Passed on by Word of Mouth From the Times of Trouble
and From Ancient Myths and Folklore Assiduously
Examined for Those Kernels of Truth That They
May Contain*

There, he thought, that at least is honest. It will put the reader on his guard that there may be errors, but giving him assurance that I have labored for the truth as best I can.

He picked up the quill again and wrote:

There is no question that at one time, perhaps five hundred years ago, Earth was possessed of an intricate and sophisticated technological civilization. Of this, nothing operational remains. The machines and the technology were destroyed, perhaps in a few months' time. And not only that, but, at least at this university, and we suppose otherwhere as well, all or most of the literary mention of the technology also was destroyed. Here, certainly, all the technological texts are gone and in many instances allusions to technology contained in other books, not technological in nature, have been edited by the ripping out of pages. What remains of the printed word concerning technology and science is only general in nature and may relate to a technology that at the time of the destruction was considered so outdated there seemed no threat in allowing it to survive. From these remaining allusions we get some hint of what the situation might have been, but not enough information to perceive the full scope of the old technology nor its impact upon the culture. Old maps of the campus show that at one time there were several buildings that were devoted to the teaching of technology and engineering. These buildings now are missing. There is a legend that the stones of which the buildings were constructed were used to build the defensive wall that now rings in the campus.

The completeness of the destruction and the apparently methodical manner in which it was carried out indicate an unreasoning rage and a fine-honed fanaticism. Seeking for cause, the first reaction is to conclude that it came about through an anger born of a hatred of what technology had brought about—the depletion of non-renewable resources, pollution of the environment, the loss of jobs resulting in massive unemployment. But this sort of reasoning, once it is examined, seems far too simplistic. On further thought, it would seem that the basic grievance that triggered the destruction must have lain in the social, economic and political systems technology had fostered.

A technological society, to be utilized to its fullest, would call for bigness—bigness in the corporate structure, in government, in finance and in the service areas. Bigness, so long as it is manageable, offers many advantages, but at a certain point in its growth, it becomes unmanageable. At about the time bigness reaches that critical size where it tends to become unmanageable, it also develops the capability to run on its own momentum and, in consequence, gets even farther out of control. Running out of control, failures and errors would creep into its operation and there would be little possibility of correction. Uncorrected, the failures and errors would be perpetuated and would feed upon themselves to achieve greater failures and even greater errors. This would happen not only in the machines themselves, but as well in top-heavy governmental and financial structures. Human managers might realize what was happening, but would be powerless in the face of it. The machines by this time would be running wild and taking along with them the complicated social and economic structures that they had made not only possible, but necessary. Long before the final crash, when the systems failed, there would have been a rising tide of anger in the land. When the crash finally came, the anger would have flashed out into an orgy of destruction, a striking back to utterly wipe out the systems and the technology that had failed, so that they never could be used again, so they would never have the chance to fail again. When this anger finished its work not only the machines wer destroyed, but the very concept of technology. That the work of destruction may have been somewhat misdirected there is no question, but it must be considered that the destruction must have been carried out by fanatics. One characteristic of the fanatic is that he must have a target against which to direct his rage. Technology, or at least the outward evidences of it, would be not only highly visible, but safe as well. A machine perforce must sit and take it. It has no way of hitting back.

That the old texts and records relating to technology were destroyed along with the machines, but only those books or the parts of those books which touched upon technology, would indicate that the sole target was technology—that the destroyers had no objection to books or learning as such. It might even be argued that they may have had a high respect for books, for even in the heat of their anger they did no damage to those which did not touch upon technology.

It makes one shudder to think of the terrible and persistent anger that must have built up to a point which made it possible to bring all this about. The misery and chaos that must have resulted from this deliberate wrecking of a way of life mankind had so laboriously built up through centuries of effort is impossible to imagine. Thousands must have died in the violence that accompanied the wrecking, and other thousands later of less violent forms of death. All that mankind had counted on and relied upon was uprooted. Anarchy replaced law and order. Communications were so thoroughly wiped out that one township scarcely knew what was happening in the next. The complex distribution system came to a halt and there was famine and starvation. Energy systems and networks were destroyed and the world went down to darkness. Medical facilities were crippled. Epidemics swept the land. We can only imagine that which happened, for there is no record left. At this late date, our darkest imagery must fail to dredge up the totality of the horror. From where we stand today, what happened would appear the result of madness rather than of simple anger, but, even so, we must realize that there must have been—must have been—seeming reason for the madness.

When the situation stabilized—if we can imagine anything like stabilization following such a catastrophe—we can only speculate on what an observer would have found. We have a few clues from present circumstances. We can see the broad outline, but that is all. In some areas, groups of farmers formed communes, holding their crop-producing acreages and their livestock by force of arms against hungry roving mobs. The cities became jungles in which pillaging combinations fought one another for the privilege of looting. Perhaps then, as now, local warlords attempted to found ruling houses, fighting with other warlords and, as now, going down one by one. In such a world—and this is true today as well as then—it was not possible for any man or band of men to achieve a power base that would serve for the building of an all-inclusive government.

The closest thing insofar as we are aware of in this area to the achievement of any sort of continuing and enduring social order is this university. Exactly how this center of relative order came about on these few acres is not known. That, once having established such order, we have endured may be explained by the fact that we are entirely defensive, at no time having sought to extend our domain or impose our will, willing to leave everyone else alone if they return the favor.

Many of the people who live beyond our walls may hate us, others will despise us as cowards who cower behind our walls, but there are some, I am sure, to whom this university has become a mystery and perhaps a magic and it may be for this reason that for the last hundred years or more we have been left alone.

The temper of communities and their intellectual environment would dictate their reaction to a situation such as the destruction of a technological society. Most would react in anger, despair and fear, taking a short-term view of the situation. A few, perhaps a very few, would be inclined to take the long-term view. In a university community the inclination would be to take a long-range view, looking not so much at the present moment but at the impact of the moment ten years from the present, or perhaps a century into the future. A university or college community, under conditions that existed before the breakup came, would have been a loosely knitted group, although perhaps more closely knitted than many of its members would have been willing to admit. All would have been inclined to regard themselves as rampant individualists, but when it came down to the crunch, most would have been brought to the realization that underlying all the fancied individualism lay a common way of thought. Instead of running and hiding, as would be the case with those who took the short-range view, a university community would have soon realized that the best course would be to stay where they were and attempt, in the midst of chaos, to form a social order based so far as possible upon the traditional values that institutions of higher learning had held throughout the years. Small areas of security and sanity, they would have reminded themselves, had persisted historically in other times of trouble. Most, when they thought of this, would have thought of the monasteries that existed as islands of tranquillity through the time of Europe's Dark Ages. Naturally, there would have been some who talked loftily of holding high the torch of learning as night fell upon the rest of mankind and there may even have been those who sincerely believed what they were saying. But, by and large, the decision would have been generally recognized as a simple matter of survival—the selection of a pattern that held a good chance of survival.

Even here, there must have been a period of stress and confusion during those early years when the destructive forces were leveling the scientific and technological centers on the campus and editing books in the libraries to eliminate all significant mention of technology. It may have been that in the heated enthusiasm of the destruction certain faculty members associated with the hated institutions may have met their deaths. The thought even occurs that certain members of the faculty may have played a part in the destruction. Reluctant as one may be to think so, it must be recognized that in that older faculty body, intense and dedicated men and women built up storied animosities, based on conflicts of principles and beliefs, with these sometimes heightened by clashing personalities.

Once the destruction was done, however, the university community, or what was left of it, must have pulled together again, burying whatever old differences that might still exist, and set about the work of establishing an enclave that stood apart from the rest of the world, designed to preserve at least some fraction of human sanity. Times would have been perilous for many years, as the protective wall built above this small segment of the campus must testify. The building of the wall would have been a long and arduous chore, but sufficiently effective leadership must have emerged to see that it was done. The university, during this period, probably was the target of many sporadic forays, although undoubtedly the dedicated looting of the city across the river and the other city to the east may have distracted some of the pressure on the campus. The contents of the stores, the shops, the homes within the cities, probably were far more attractive than anything the campus had to offer.

Since there are no communications with the world outside the wall and all the news we get are the tales told by occasional travelers, we cannot pretend to know what may be happening otherwhere than here. Many events may be taking place of which we know nothing. But in the small area that we do know, or of which we have some fragmentary knowledge, the highest level of social organization seems to be the tribe or those farming communes, with one which we have set up rudimentary trade relations. Immediately to the east and west of us, in what once were fair and pleasant cities, now largely gone to ruin, are several tribes grubbing a bare existence from the land and occasionally warring with one another over imagined grievances or to gain some coveted territory (although only God knows why coveted) or simply for the illusionary glory that may be gained from combat. To the north is a farm commune or perhaps a dozen families with which we have made trade accommodations, their produce serving to augment the vegetables we grow in gardens and our potato patches. For this food, we pay in trinketry—beadwork, badly constructed jewelry, leather goods—which they, in their simple-mindedness, are avid to obtain for their personal adornment. To such an extent have we fallen—that a once-proud university should manufacture and trade trinkets for its food.

At one time, family groups may have held on to small homesteads, hiding from the world. Many of these homesteads no longer exist, either wiped out or their members forced to join a tribe for the protection that it offered. And there are always the nomads, the roving, far-wandering bands with their cattle and their horses, at times sending out war parties to pillage, although there now is little enough to pillage. Such is the state of the world as we are acquainted with it; such is our own state, and sorry as it may be, in certain ways we are far better off than many of the others.

To a certain small extent we have kept alive the flame of learning. Our children are taught to read and write and cipher. Those who wish may gain additional rudimentary learning and there are books to be read, of course, tons of books, and from the reading of those, many in the community are fairly well informed. Reading and writing are skills that few have today, even those basic skills being lost through the lack of anyone to teach them. Occasionally, there are a few who make their way to us to gain the little education we can offer, but not many, for education apparently is not highly regarded. Some of those who come continue to stay on with us and thus some diversity is added to our gene pool, a diversity of which we stand in need. It may be that some of those who come to us, professing a wish for education, may actually come to seek the security of our walls, fleeing the rough justice of their fellows. This we do not mind; we take them in. So long as they come in peace and keep the peace once they are here, they are welcome.

Anyone with half an eye, however, should be able to see that we have lost much of our effectiveness as an educational institution. We can teach the simple things, but since the second generation of the enclave's establishment, there has been none qualified to teach anything approaching a higher education. We have no teachers of physics or chemistry, of philosophy or psychology, of medicine or of many other disciplines. Even if we had, there would be little need. Who in this environment needs physics or chemistry? What is the use of medicine if drugs are unobtainable, if there is no equipment for therapy of surgery?

We have often idly speculated among ourselves whether there may be other colleges or universities still existing in the same manner as we exist. It would seem reasonable that there might be, but we've had no word of them. In turn, we have not attempted to find out and have not seen fit to unduly advertise our presence.

In books that I have read, there are contained many considered and logical prophesies that such a catastrophe as came about would come to pass. But, in all cases, war was foreseen as the cause of it. Armed with incalculable engines of destruc-

tion, the major powers of that olden day possessed the capability to annihilate one another (and, in a smaller sense, the world) in a few hours' time. This, however, did not come about. There is no evidence of the ravages of war and there are no legends that tell of such a war.

From all indications that we have at this date, the collapse of civilization came about because of an outrage on the part of what must have been a substantial portion of the populace against the kind of world that technology had created, although the outrage, in many instances, may have been misdirected. . . .

4

Dwight Cleveland Montrose was a lithe, lean man, his face a seasoned leather, the brownness of it set off by the snow-white hair, the bristling grayness of the mustache, the heavy eyebrows that were exclamation points above the bright eyes of washed-out blue. He sat straight upright in the chair, shoving away the dinner plate he had polished clean. He wiped his mustache with a napkin and pushed back from the table.

"How did the potatoes go today?" he asked.

"I finished hoeing them," said Cushing. "I think this is the last time. We can lay them by. Even a spell of drought shouldn't hurt them too much now."

"You work too hard," said Nancy. "You work harder than you should."

She was a bright little birdlike woman, shrunken by her years, a wisp of a woman with sweetness in her face. She looked fondly at Cushing in the flare of candlelight.

"I like to work," he told her. "I enjoy it. And a little proud of it, perhaps. Other people can do other things. I grow good potatoes."

"And now," said Monty, brusquely, brushing at his mustache, "I suppose you will be leaving."

"Leaving!"

"Tom," he said, "you've been with us how long? Six years, am I right?"

"Five years," said Cushing. "Five years last month."

"Five years," said Monty. "Five years. That's long enough to know you. As close as we all have been, long enough to know you. And during the last few months, you've been jumpy as a cat. I've never asked you why. We, Nancy and I, never asked you why. On anything at all."

"No, you never did," said Cushing. "There must have been times when I was a trial. . . ."

"Never a trial," said Monty. "No, sir, never that. We had a son, you know. . . ."

"He was with us just a while," said Nancy. "Six years. That was all. If he had lived, he'd be the same age as you are now."

"Measles," said Monty. "Measles, for the love of God. There was a time when men knew how to deal with measles, how to prevent them. There was a time when measles were almost never heard of."

"There were sixteen others," Nancy said, remembering. "Seventeen, with John. All with measles. It was a terrible winter. The worst we've ever known."

"I am sorry," Cushing said.

"The sorrow is over now," said Monty. "The surface sorrow, that is. There is a deeper sorrow that will be with us all our lives. We speak very seldom of it because we do not want you to think you are standing in his stead, that you are taking his place, that we love you because of him."

"We love you," said Nancy, speaking gently, "because

21

you're Thomas Cushing. No one but yourself. We sorrow less, I think, because of you. Some of the old-time hurt is gone because of you. Tom, we owe you more than the two of us can tell you."

"We owe you enough," said Monty, "to talk as we do now—a strange kind of talk, indeed. It was becoming intolerable, you know. You not saying anything to us because you thought we'd not understand, held to us because of a mistaken loyalty. We knowing from the things you did and the way you acted what you had in mind and yet compelled to hold our peace because we did not think we should be the ones who brought what you were thinking out into the open. We had feared that if we said anything about it, you might think we wanted you to leave, and you know well enough that we never would want that. But this foolishness has gone on long enough and now we think that we should tell you that we hold enough affection for you to let you go if you feel you really have to, or if you only want to. If you must leave us, we would not have you go with guilt, feeling you have run out on us. We've watched you the last few months, wanting to tell us, shying away from telling us. Nervous as a cat. Itching to go free."

"It's not that," said Cushing. "Not itching to go free."

"It's this Place of Going to the Stars," said Monty. "I would suppose that's it. If I were a younger man, I think that I'd be going, too. Although, I'm not sure that I could force myself to go. I think that through the centuries we people in this university have become agoraphobes. All of us have stayed so long, huddled on this campus, that none of us ever thinks of going anywhere."

"Can I take this to mean," asked Cushing, "that you are trying to say you think there may be something to this business Wilson wrote down in his notes—that there could be a Place of Going to the Stars?"

"I do not know," said Monty. "I would not even try to guess. Ever since you showed me the notes and told me of your finding them I have been thinking on it. Not just wool-gathering, romantic thoughts about how exciting it might be if there were such a place, but trying to weigh the factors that would make such a situation true or false, and I am forced to tell you that I think it might be possible. We do know that men went out into the solar system. We know they went to the Moon and Mars. And in light of this, we must ask ourselves if they would have been satisfied with only Moon and Mars. I don't think they would have been. Given the capability, they'd have left the solar system. Given time, they would have gained that capability. We have no hint of whether they did gain the capability because those last few hundred years before the Collapse are hidden from us. It is those few hundred years that were excised from the books. The people who brought about the Collapse wanted to erase all memory of those few centuries and we have no way to know what might have happened during that long span of time. But judging from the progress that men had made during those years that we do know about, that were left to us to read, it seems to me almost certain that they would have gained deep-space capability."

"We had so hoped that you would stay with us," said Nancy. "We had thought it might be only a passing fancy, and that in time you would get over it. But now it is apparent to us that you will not get over it. Monty and I talked it over, not once, but many times. We were convinced finally that for some compelling reason you did wish to go."

"There is one thing that bothers me," said Cushing. "You are right, of course. I've been trying to screw up my courage to tell you. I cringed from it, but each time that I decided not to go, there was something in me that told me I had to go. The thing that bothers me is that I don't know why. I tell myself it's the

Place of Going to the Stars and then I wonder if, deep down, it may be something else. Is it, I ask myself, the wolf blood still in me? For three years before I came knocking at the gate of the university, I was a woods runner. I think I told you that."

"Yes," said Monty. "Yes, you told us that."

"But nothing more," said Cushing. "You never asked. Neither of you ever asked. I wonder now why I never told you."

"You need not tell us now," said Nancy, gently. "We have no need to know."

"But now I have a need to tell you," Cushing said. "The story is a short one. There were three of us: my mother and my grandfather—my mother's father—and myself. My father, too, but I don't remember him. Maybe just a little. A big man with black whiskers that tickled when he kissed me."

He'd not thought of it for years, not really thought of it, forcing himself not to think of it, but now, quite suddenly, he saw it clear as day. A little coulee that ran back from the Mississippi, in that land of tangled hills that lay a week's walking to the south. A small sand-bottomed creek ran through the narrow meadowlands that lay between the sharply sloping bluffs, fed by a large spring that gushed out of the sandstone at the coulee's head, where the hills pinched in. Beside the spring was home—a small house gray with the oldness of its wood, a soft gray that blended in with the shadow of the hills and trees so it could not be seen, if one did not know that it was there, until one almost stumbled on it. A short distance off stood two other small gray buildings as difficult to see as was the house—a dilapidated barn that housed two crowbait horses, three cows and a bull, and the chicken house, which was falling down. Below the house lay a garden and potato patch; and up a small side valley that angled out from the coulee, a small patch of corn.

Here he had lived for his first sixteen years, and in all that time, he remembered no more than a dozen people who had come visiting. They had no nearby neighbors and the place was off the path of the wandering tribes that went up and down the river valley. The coulee mouth was only one of many mouths of similar coulees, and a small one at that, and it had no attraction for anyone who might be passing by. It had been a quiet place, drowsing through the years, but colorful, with a flood of crab apple and wild plum and cherry blossoms clothing it in softness every spring. Again in autumn the oaks and maples flamed into raging fires of brilliant red and yellow. At times the hills were covered by hepaticas, violets, trout lilies, sweet william, bloodroot, spring beauty and yellow lady's slipper. There had been fishing in the creek, and also fishing in the river if one wanted to go that far to fish. But mostly fishing in the creek, where there might be caught, without too great an effort, the small, delicious brook trout. There had been squirrels and rabbits for the pot and, if one could move silently enough and shoot an arrow well enough, ruffed grouse and perhaps even quail, although quail were small and quick and tiny targets for a bow. But Thomas Cushing, at times, had brought home quail. He had used a bow and arrow from the time he had been big enough to toddle, having been taught its use by his grandfather, who was a master of it. In the fall the coons had come down from the hills to raid the corn patch, and though they took part of the crop, they paid heavily for it, returning in their meat and hides far more than the value of the corn they took. For there always had been coon dogs at the cabin, sometimes only one or two, sometimes many of them; and when the coons came down to raid, Tom and his grandfather had gone out with the dogs that trailed the coons and caught them or cornered them or treed them. When they had been treed, Tom had climbed the tree, with a bow in one hand and two arrows in his teeth, going slowly, searching for the coon, clinging to a limb somewhere above him and silhouetted against the night sky. It had been tricky climbing and tricky shooting, propped against the trunk of the tree to shoot. Sometimes the coon would get away and other times it wouldn't.

It was his grandfather whom it now seemed he could remember best—always an old man with grizzled hair and beard, sharp nose, mean and squinting eyes—for he was a mean man, but never mean with Tom. Old and tough and mean, a man who knew the woods and hills and river. A profane man who swore bitterly at his aching and arthritic joints, who cursed the fate of growing old, who brooked no foolishness and no arrogance except his own foolishness and arrogance. A fanatic when it came to tools and weapons and to domestic animals. Although a horse might be roundly cursed, it was never flogged, never mistreated, well taken care of—for a horse would be hard to replace. One might be bought, of course, if one knew where to go; or stolen, and stealing, as a rule, was easier than buying, but either took a great deal of time and effort and there was a certain danger in either of them. Weapons you must not use lightly. You shot no arrow uselessly. You shot at a mark to improve your skill; the only other time you shot was when you shot to kill. You learned to use a knife the way it should be used and you took care of knives, for knives were hard to obtain. The same thing with tools. When you were through with plowing, you cleaned and polished and greased the plow and stored it in the barn loft, for a plow must be guarded against rust—it must last through many generations. Harness for the horses was oiled and cobbled and kept in good repair. When you were finished with your hoeing, you washed and dried the hoe before putting it away. When haying was done the scythe was cleaned, sharpened, and coated with grease and hung back in its place. There could be no sloppiness, no forgetting. It was a way of life. To make do with what you had, to take care of it, to guard against its loss, to use it correctly, so that no damage would be done to it.

His father Tom could recall only vaguely. He had always thought of him as having been lost, for that was the story he'd been told when he was old enough to understand. It seemed, however, that no one had actually known what had happened to him. One spring morning, according to the story, he had set out for the river with a fish spear in hand and a bag slung across his shoulder. It was time for the carp to spawn, coming into the shoals of the river valley's sloughs and lakes to lay and fertilize their eggs. In the frenzy of the season they had no fear in them and were easy prey. Each year, as that year, Tom's father had gone to the river when the carp were running, perhaps making several trips, coming home each time bowed down by the bulging sack full of carp slung across his shoulder, using the reversed spear as a walking stick to help himself along. Brought home, the carp were scaled and cleaned, cut into fillets and smoked to provide food throughout a good part of the summer months.

But this time he did not return. By late afternoon, Tom's mother and the old grandfather set out to search for him, Tom riding on his grandfather's shoulder. They came back late at night, having found nothing. The next day the grandfather went out again and this time found the spear, abandoned beside a shallow lake in which the carp still rolled, and a short distance off, the sack, but nothing else. There was no sign of Tom's father, no indication of what had happened to him. He had vanished and there was no trace of him and since that time there had been no word of him.

Life went on much as it had before, a little harder now since there were fewer to grub a living from the land. However, they did not do too badly. There was always food to eat and wood to burn and hides to tan for clothing and for footwear. One horse died—of old age, more than likely—and the old man went away and was gone for ten days or more, then returned with two horses. He never said how he had got them and no one ever asked. They knew he must have stolen them, for he had taken nothing with him that would have served to buy them. They were young and strong and it was a good thing that he'd got the two of them, for a short time later, the other old horse died as well and two horses were needed to plow the field and gardens, haul the wood and get in the hay. By this time, Tom was old enough to help—ten years or so—and one of the things he remembered vividly was helping his grandfather skin the two dead horses. He had blubbered while he did it, trying to hide the blubbers from his grandfather and later, alone, had wept bitterly, for he had loved those horses. But it would have been a waste not to take their hides, and in their kind of life there was nothing ever wasted.

When Tom was fourteen, his mother sickened in a hard and terrible winter when snow lay deep and blizzard after blizzard came hammering down across the hills. She had taken to her bed, gasping for breath, wheezing as she breathed. The two of them had taken care of her, the mean, irascible old man transformed into a soul of tenderness. They rubbed her throat with warm goose grease, kept in a bottle in a cabinet for just such an emergency, and wrapped her throat in a cherished piece of flannel cloth to help the goose grease do its work. They put hot bricks at her feet to keep her warm and the grandfather cooked a syrup of onions on the stove, keeping it at the back of the stove so it would stay warm, and fed the syrup to her to alleviate the soreness of her throat. One night, tired with watching, Tom had fallen asleep. He was wakened by the old man. "Boy," he'd said, "your mother's gone." And having said that, the old man turned away so that Tom could not see his tears.

In the first gray of morning light they went out and shoveled away the snow beneath an ancient oak where Tom's mother had loved to sit, looking down the coulee, then built a fire to thaw the ground so they could dig a grave. In the spring, with much labor, they had hauled three huge boulders, one by one, on a stoneboat, and had placed them on the grave—to mark it and to keep it safe against the wolves that, now the frost was gone, might try to dig it up.

Life went on again, although it seemed to Tom that some-thing had gone out of the old grandfather. He still did a moderate amount of cussing, but some of the eloquent fire had gone out of it. He spent more time in the rocking chair on the porch than he ever had before. Tom did most of the work now, the old man dawdling about. The grandfather seemed to want to talk, as if talk might fill the emptiness that had fallen on him. Hour after hour, he and Tom would talk, sitting on the porch, or when the nights grew chill and winter came, sitting in front of the blazing fire. It was the grandfather who did most of the talking, dredging from his almost eighty years of life tales of events that had taken place many years before, not all of them, perhaps, entirely true, but each incident more than likely based on an actual happening that could have been interesting in itself without all the extra trappings. The story about the time when he had gone traipsing to the west and had killed an arrow-wounded grizzly with a knife (a story that Tom, even at his tender years, accepted with a grain of salt); the story of a classic horse-trading deal in which (as change of pace) the old man got handsomely swindled; the story about the monstrous catfish that it took three hours to land; the story about the time, on one of his fabulous trips, he became entangled in a short-lived war fought by two tribes for no reason whatsoever that could be adequately explained, fighting most likely just for the hell of it; and the story about a university (whatever a university might be) far to the north, surrounded by a wall and inhabited by a curious breed that was termed, with some contempt "egghead," although the old man was quite content to admit that he had no idea what an egghead was, hazarding a guess that those who used the term had no idea of its meaning either, but were simply using a term of contempt that had come out of the dim and ancient past. Listening to his grandfather through the long afternoons and evenings, the boy began to see a different man, a younger man, shining through the meanness of the older man. Seeing, perhaps, that the shifty-eyed meanness was little more than a mask that he had put on as a defense against old age, which he apparently considered the final great indignity that a man was forced to undergo.

But not for a great deal longer. In the summer that Tom was sixteen he came home at noon from plowing corn to find the old man fallen from his rocking chair, sprawling on the porch, no longer suffering any indignity other than the indignity of death, if death can be thought of as an indignity. Tom dug the grave and buried him beneath the same oak tree where the mother had been buried, and hauled boulders, smaller boulders this time, for he was the only one left to handle them, to be piled upon the grave.

"You grew up fast," said Monty.

"Yes," said Cushing, "I suppose I did."

"And then you took to the woods."

"Not right off," said Cushing. "There was the farm, you see, and the animals. I couldn't run off and leave the animals. They get so they depend on you. You don't just walk away and leave them. There was this family I had heard of, on a ridge about ten miles away. It was hard scratching there. A poor spring they had to walk to for their water about a mile away. The land stony and thin. A tough clay that was hard to work. They stayed there because there were buildings to give them warmth and shelter, but there wasn't much else. The house stood there on the ridge, swept by every wind that came along. The crops were poor and they were out where any wandering band could see them. So I went to see the family and we made a deal. They took over my farm and animals, with me getting half the increase from my livestock, if there was any increase and if I ever came back to claim it. They moved down to the coulee and I took off. I couldn't stay. There were too many memories there. I saw too many people and I heard too many voices. I had to have something to do to keep busy. I could have stayed on the farm, of course, and there'd have been work to do, but not enough work and wondering why I did it and looking at the two graves and thinking back. I don't believe I reasoned it out at the time. I just knew I had to walk away, but before I went, I had to be sure there was someone to care for the animals. I suppose I could just have turned them loose, but that wouldn't have been right. They would have wondered what had happened. They get used to people and they sort of count on them. They are lost without them.

"Nor do I think I even tried to figure out what I would do once I was free of the farm. I just took to the woods. I was well trained for it. I knew the woods and river. I had grown up with them. It was a wild, free life, but at first I drove myself. Anything to keep busy, to put the miles behind me. But finally

I eased off and drifted. I had no responsibility. I could go anywhere I wished, do anything I wished. Over the course of the first year I fell in with two other runners, young twerps like myself. We made a good team. We went far south and roamed around a bit, then we wandered back. We spent some time one spring and summer along the Ohio. That's good country to be in. But as time went on, we drifted apart. I wanted to go north and the others didn't. I'd got to thinking about the story my grandfather told about the university and I was curious. From things I'd picked up I knew it was a place where you could learn to read and write and I thought those might be handy things to have. In one tribe down south—in Alabama, maybe, I can't be sure—I found an old man who could read. He read the Bible mostly and did a lot of preaching. I thought what a fine thing that would be, not the Bible, you understand, nor the preaching, but being able to read."

"It must have seemed a good life," Monty said. "You enjoyed it. It helped to wipe away the memories. Buried them to some extent; softened them, perhaps."

Cushing nodded. "I suppose it was a good life. I still think back on it and recall how good it was, remembering the good things only. Not all of it was good."

"And now perhaps you want to go again just to see how good it was. To find out if it was as good as you remembered it. And the Place of Going to the Stars, of course."

"The Place of Stars," said Cushing, "has haunted me ever since I found Wilson's notes. I keep asking myself, what if there should be such a place and no one went to find it?"

"You plan to be leaving, then?"

"Yes, I think I will. But I'll be back. I won't stay away forever. Only until I've found the Place or know it can't be found."

"You'll be going west. Have you ever gone into the West?"
Cushing shook his head.

"It's different from the woods," said Monty. "When you get out a hundred miles or so, you come to open prairie. You'll have to watch yourself. We have word, remember, that there is something stirring out there. Some warlord pulling some of the tribes together and going on the prod. They'll be heading east, I would imagine, although one can never know what goes on in a nomad's head."

"I'll watch myself," said Cushing.

5

The Team rolled along the boulevard, as they did each morning. It was their time for cogitation, for the absorption and classification of all that they had learned or sensed or otherwise acquired the day before.

The sky was clear, without a cloud in sight, and once the star got up it would be another scorcher. Except for the birds that chirped discontentedly in the scraggly trees and the little rodents that went skittering through the tunnels in the grass, there was nothing else astir. Rank grass and lusty weeds grew in the pavement cracks. Time-grimed statuary and no-longer-operative fountains lurked in the jungle of unattended shrubbery. Beyond the statuary and the fountains the great piles of the buildings went up against the sky.

"I have thought much upon the situation," said #1, "and still I fail to comprehend the logic of the Ancient and Revered in pretending to be hopeful. By all the criteria that we have developed in our millennia of study throughout the galaxy, the dominant race upon this planet is lost beyond redemption. The race has gone through basically the same process that we have witnessed elsewhere. They built their civilization without realizing the inherent flaw that brought them to destruction. And yet the A and R insists that what has happened is no more than a temporary setback. He tells us that there have been many other setbacks in the history of the race and that in each case it has triumphed over them and emerged in greater strength than it knew before. I sometimes wonder if his thinking could be twisted by the loyalty he still carries in this precious race of his. Certainly one can understand his ingrained faith in these creatures, but the evidence all would indicate the faith is wrongly placed. Either he is unconsciously being intellectually dishonest or is naive beyond our estimation of him."

#2, who had been gazing up into the sky, now floated a group of eyes down across the smooth ball of his body and stared in some disbelief at his companion.

"I am surprised at you," he said. "You surely must be jesting or are under greater strain that I had thought you were. The A and R is neither naive nor dishonest. On the face of what we know, we must accord him the honor of believing in his sincerity. What is more likely is that he has some knowledge that he has chosen not to communicate to us, perhaps an unconscious knowledge that we have failed, with all our investigation and our probing, to uncover. We could have erred in our assessment of the race. . . ."

"I think," said #1, "that is quite unlikely. The situation fits a classic pattern that we have found time and time again. There are, I grant you, some disturbing factors here, but the pattern is unmistakable. We know beyond any question that the race upon this planet has arrived at the classic end of a classic situation. It has gone into its last decline and will not recover."

"I would be inclined to agree with you," said #2, "except for certain doubts. I am inclined to believe that there are hidden factors we have not recognized, or worse, factors that we have glimpsed and paid no attention to, considering them to be only secondary."

"We have found our answer," #1 said, stubbornly, "and we should long since have been gone from here. Our time is wasted. This history is but little different from the many other histories that we have collected. What is it that worries you so much?"

"The robots, for one thing," said #2. "Have we accorded them the full consideration they deserve, or have we written them off too hastily? By writing them off too quickly, we may have missed the full significance of them and the impact they may have had—or still may have—upon the situation. For they are, in fact, an extension of the race that created them. Perhaps a significant extension. They may not, as we have told ourselves, be playing out previously programmed and now meaningless roles. We have been unable to make any sense out of our interviews with them, but—"

"We have not, in a certain sense, actually interviewed them," #1 pointed out. "They have thrust themselves upon us, each one intent on telling us meaningless stories that have no coherence in them. There is no pattern in what they tell us. We don't know what to believe or if we should believe any of it at all. All of it is gibberish. And we must realize, as well, that these robots can be no more than they seem. They are machines and, at times, atrociously clumsy machines. As such, they are only an embodied symptom of that decay which is characteristic of all technological societies. They are a stupid lot and, what is more, arrogant. Of all possible combinations, stupidity and arrogance is the worst that can be found. The basic badness of them is that they feed on one another."

"You generalize too much," protested #2. "Much of what

you say may be quite correct, but there are exceptions. The Ancient and Revered is neither arrogant nor stupid, and though somewhat more sophisticated than the others, he is still a robot."

"I agree," said #1, "that the A and R is neither arrogant nor stupid. He is, by every measure, a polished and well-mannered gentleman, and yet, as I pointed out, he fails of making sense. He is involved in fuzzy thinking, basing his viewpoints on a slender reed of hope that is unsupported by any evidence—that, in fact, flies in the face of evidence. We are trained observers with a long record of performance. We have existed for a much longer span of time than the A and R and during that existence we have always striven for strict objectivity—something that is alien to the A and R, with all his talk of faith and hope."

"I would judge," said #2, "that it is time for us to cease this discussion. We have fallen into crude bickering, which will get us nowhere. It is amazing to me, and a source of sorrow, that after all the time we have worked together we still are capable of falling into such a state. I take it as a warning that in this particular study there is something very wrong. It indicates that we still have failed to reach that state of crystal perfection we attempt to put into our work and the reason for that, in this study, must be that there are underlying truths we have failed to come to grips with and that in our subconscious they rise up to plague us."

"I do not," said #1, "agree with you at all, but what you say about the futility of continuing this discussion is very solemn truth. So let us, for the moment, derive whatever enjoyment we may from our morning stroll."

6

Cushing had crossed the river, using a crudely constructed log raft to protect his bow and quiver and to help him in his swimming. He had started opposite the wall of the university and allowed the swift current to carry him downstream as he kicked for the other shore, calculating in his mind that he would reach it at about the point where a creek cut through the walls of the bluff. This way there'd be no bluffs to climb, the valley of the creek giving him easy access across the southern limits of the city. He'd not been in this part of the city before and he wondered what he'd find, although he was fairly certain it would not be a great deal different from those fringe sections of the city he had seen—a tangle of olden houses falling in upon themselves or already fallen, faint trails leading in all directions, the remnants of ancient streets where, even to this day, the hard surface of the paving kept them free of heavy growth.

Later on the moon would rise, but now blackness lay across the land. Out on the river the choppiness of the water had caught and shattered into tiny rainbows the faint glimmer of the stars, but here, underneath the trees that grew along the left bank of the creek at the point where it joined the river, the reflected starlight could no longer be seen.

He retrieved the quiver from the raft and slung it across his shoulder, shrugged into the shoulder harness that supported his small backpack, picked up the bow, then nudged the raft with a cautious toe out into the river. He crouched at the water's edge and watched until, in half a dozen feet or so, the raft was swallowed by the darkness and the river. The sweep of current from the inflowing creek would carry it out into the center of the stream and there'd be nothing to show that someone had crossed the river under the cover of night.

Once the raft had disappeared, he continued in his crouch, all senses alert. Somewhere to the north a dog was barking with determination, barking with a steady cadence—not excited, not even sensible, as if it were its duty to be barking. Something across the creek was rustling in the bushes, cautiously but purposefully. An animal, Cushing knew, not a human. More than likely a coon come down off the bluff to fish for clams. Mosquitoes buzzed about his head, but he paid them no attention. Out in the potato patch, day after day, he had become accustomed to mosquitoes and their venom. They were no more than a nuisance, with their high-pitched, vicious singing.

Satisfied that he had crossed unobserved, he rose and made his way along the shingle at the river's edge, reaching the creek and stepping into it. The water came no higher than his knees and he began working his way upstream, on guard against sudden dropoffs.

His eyes by now had become somewhat adapted to the dark and he could make out the blacker bulk of trees, the faint gleam of rapidly running water. He did not hurry. He felt his way along, making no noise. Low-hanging branches caught at him and he ducked under them or held them to one side.

A mile or so from where he had entered the creek, he came to what he made out to be an old stone bridge. Leaving the water, he climbed the incline to the bridge to reach the street that at one time had passed over it. Beneath his moccasins he could feel the broken hardness of the paving, covered now by grass and weeds and hemmed in by briars. To the north the dog went on with its chugging and now, to the south and west, other distant dogs had chimed in to answer. Off in the bushes to his right, a bird twittered in alarm, startled by some birdish fear. Through the treetops to the east Cushing saw the first flush of the rising moon.

He went north until he found an intersecting street and then turned to his left, traveling west. He doubted that he could clear the city before morning light, but he wanted to be as far along as he could manage. Well before dawn he would have to find a place to hole up during daylight hours.

He was surprised to find himself, now that he was on his way, filled with a strange exhilaration. Freedom, he thought. Was that it, after all the years—the freedom—that exhilarated him? Was this the way, he wondered, that the ancient American long hunters had felt once they had shaken the dust of the eastern settlements off their feet? Was this the feeling of the old-time mountain man, equally mythical as the long hunters, when he had headed for the beaver streams? Was this the feeling that had been experienced by the astronauts when they had pointed the noses of their ships toward the distant stars? If they had, in fact, pointed at any stars at all.

Occasionally, as he slipped along, he caught glimpses, on either side, of dark bulks looming among the trees. As the moon moved higher in the sky, he saw that the bulks were what was left of houses. Some of them still held the shape of houses and others were little more than piles of debris, not yet having settled into mounds or fallen into basements. He was, he knew, moving through a residential section and tried to picture in his mind what it might have looked like at another time—a tree-lined street with houses sitting, new and shining, in the greenness of their lawns. And the people in them—over there a doctor, across the street a lawyer, just down the street the owner of a hardware store. Children and dogs playing on the lawn, a mailman trudging on his rounds, a ground vehicle parked beside the curb. He shrugged, thinking of it, wondering how nearly he was right, how much the picture he was building in his mind might be romanticized. There had been pictures of such streets in the old files of magazines he'd read, but were these, he wondered, no more than highly selective pictures, unrepresentative of the general scene.

The moonlight was stronger now and he could see that the street he moved along was filled with clumps of small bushes and with patches of briars through which a narrow trail snaked along, weaving from side to side to avoid the heavier growth that had intruded on the street. A deer path, he wondered, or was it one primarily used by men? If it were a man path, he should not be on it. He pondered that, deciding to stay on it. On it he could cover a fair amount of ground; off to one side of it, his way impeded by heavy growths of trees, fallen timber, the old houses and, worse, the gaping basements where houses had once stood, his progress would be slowed.

Something caught his foot and tripped him, throwing him off balance. As he went down, something raked against his cheek, and behind him he heard a heavy thud. Twisting around from where he had landed in the briars, he saw the feathered shaft of an arrow protruding from a tree to one side of the twisting trail. A set, he told himself; for Christ's sake, a set, and he had blundered into it. A few inches either way and he'd

41

have had an arrow in his shoulder or his throat. A trip across the path to trigger a bended bow, the arrow held in place by a peg. Cold fear and anger filled him. A set for what? For deer, or man? What he should do, he thought, was wait here, hidden, until the owner of the set came at morning light to see what he had bagged, then put an arrow in him to ensure he'd never set such a trap again. But he didn't have the time to do it; by morning light he must be far from here.

He rose from the briars and moved off the street, plowing through rank growths of brush. Off the street the going was slower. It was darker among the trees, the moonlight blocked by dense foliage, and, as he had anticipated, there were obstacles.

A short time later he heard a sound that brought him to a halt, poised in mid-stride, waiting to hear the sound again. When it came, in the space of a heartbeat or two, he knew what it was: the soft mutter of a drum. He waited and the sound came again, louder now and with the drumrolls longer. Then it fell silent, only to take up again, louder and more insistent, not simply the tatooing ruffle of a single drum but more drums now, with the somber booming of a bigger drum marking off the ruffles.

He puzzled over it. He had struck across the city's southern edge, believing that by doing so he would swing wide of any tribal encampment. Although, so far as that was concerned, he had been foolish to think so. One could never tell where a camp might be. The tribes, while staying in the confines of the city, moved around a great deal. When the vicinity of one camping ground became too fouled for comfort, the tribe would move down the street a ways.

The drums were gaining strength and volume. They were, he calculated, some distance ahead of him and slightly to the north. Some big doings, he told himself, grinning in the dark. A celebration of some sort, perhaps a commemorative notice of some tribal anniversary. He started moving once again. The thing for him to do was get out of here, to pay no attention to the drums and continue on his way.

As he slogged along, keeping off the clearer paths of the one-time streets, the noise of the drumming grew. There was in it now a blood-curdling savagery that had not been evidenced at the start. Listening to it, Cushing shivered, and yet, chilling as it was, it held a certain fascination. From time to time, interspersed between the drumbeats, he could hear a shouting and the yapping of dogs. In another mile or so he detected the flare of fires, slightly to the north and west, reflected off the sky.

He stopped to gauge the situation better. Whatever was going on was taking place just over the brow of the hill that reared up to his right—much closer than he first had judged it. Perhaps, he told himself, he should angle to the south, putting more distance between himself and whatever might be going on. There might be sentries out and there was no sense in taking the chance of bumping into them.

But he made no move. He stood there, with his back against a tree, staring up the hill, listening to the drumming and the shouting. Maybe he should know, he told himself, what was happening just beyond the hill. It would take no time at all. He could sneak up the hill and have a look, then be on his way again. No one would spot him. He'd keep a close outlook for sentries. The moon was out, of course, but here, underneath the heavy foliage of the trees, its light was tricky and uncertain at the best.

Almost before he knew it he had started up the hill, moving at a crouch, sometimes on hands and knees, seeking the deeper shadows, watching for any movement, slithering up the slope, the low-hanging branches sliding noiselessly off his buckskins.

There is trouble brewing, Monty had reminded him, trouble in the west. Some nomad band that had suddenly been seized with the thirst for conquest, and probably moving east. Could it be, he wondered, that the city tribes had spotted such a movement and were now in the process of whipping themselves into a warlike frenzy?

Now that he was near the brow of the hill, his caution increased. He slid along from one deep shadow to another, studying the ground ahead before he made any move. Beyond the hill the bedlam grew. The drums rolled and thundered and the yelling never ceased. The dogs kept up their excited barking.

Finally he reached the ridgetop, and there, below him, in a bowl-like valley, he saw the ring of fires and the dancing, yelling figures. In the center of the circle of fires stood a gleaming pyramid that caught and reflected the light of the leaping flames.

A pyramid of skulls, he thought—a pyramid of polished human skulls—but even as he thought it, he remembered something else and knew that he was wrong. He was looking at, he knew, not human skulls but the skulls of long-dead robots, the shining, polished brain cases of robots whose bodies had gone to rust centuries before.

Wilson had written of such pyramids, he recalled, and had speculated on the mysticism or the symbolism that might be behind the collection and display of them.

He hunkered close against the ground and felt a shiver growing in him, a shiver that reached forward across the old, gone centuries to fasten icy fingers on him. He paid little attention to the leaping, shouting figures, his attention fas-

tened on the pyramid. It had about it a barbaric aura that left
him cold and weak and he began inching back, carefully down
the hill, moving as cautiously as he had before, but now driven
by a gripping fear.

Near the foot of the hill he rose and headed south and west,
still moving warily, but in a hurry now. Behind him the drumming and the shouting faded until it was no more than a
murmur in the distance. But he still drove himself.

The first paleness of dawn was in the eastern sky when he
found a place to hole up for the day. It was what appeared to be
an old estate, set above a lake and situated on a piece of ground
enclosed by a still-standing metal fence. Glancing eastward
across the lake, he tried to pinpoint the spot where the tribe
had held its dance, but except for a thin trickle of smoke, he
could make out nothing. The house was a stone and brick
structure and so thoroughly masked by trees that he did not see
it until he had made his way through a broken place in the
fence and was almost upon it. Chimneys sprouted from both
ends of it and a sagging portico, half collapsed, ran along its
front. Behind it stood several small brick buildings, half ob-
scured by trees. Grass grew tall and here and there beds of
perennials, some of them in bloom, had persisted through the
ages since the last people had occupied the house.

He scouted the area in the early dawn. There was no evidence that anyone had visited the place in recent days. There
were no paths, no trails, broken through the grass. Centuries
before, the place must have been looted, and now there would
be no reason for anyone to come back here.

He did not approach the house, contented to view it from
the shelter of the trees. Satisfied that it was deserted, he
sought a place where he could hide himself, finding it in a thick
cluster of lilac trees that had spread over a comparatively wide

area. On hands and knees he wormed his way deep into the thicket until he came to a spot near the center where there was room enough to lie down.

He rose to a sitting position, propping his back against a thick tangle of lilac trunks. He was engulfed in the greenery of the clump. It would be impossible for anyone passing by to know that he was there. He unshipped the quiver and laid it, with the bow, alongside him, then slipped off the backpack and untied the thongs that closed it. From it he took a slab of jerked meat and with his knife belt cut off a piece of it. It was tough to chew and had little flavor, but it was good food for the trail. It was light of weight, would not spoil, and was life sustaining— good solid beef, dried until there was little moisture left. He sat and munched it, feeling the tension draining out of him, draining, it seemed, into the ground on which he sat, leaving him tired and relaxed. Here, he thought, was momentary peace and refuge against the day. The worst was over now. He had crossed the city and was now in its western reaches.

He had faced the dangers of the city and had come through unscathed. Although, in thinking this, he realized, he was deluding himself. There had never been any actual danger, no threat directed at him. The set trap had been an accident. The intended game, most likely, had been a bear or deer and he had simply blundered into it. It had posed a danger born of his own carelessness. In a hostile, or even unknown, land a man did not travel trails. He stayed well off them, at worst paralleling them and keeping eyes and ears well open. Three years of woods-running had taught him this and he should have remembered it. He warned himself that he must not forget again. The years at the university had lulled him into a false security, had changed his way of thinking. If he was going to get through this foray into the west, he must revert to his old way of caution.

Sneaking up to take a look at the dance or celebration or

whatever it might have been had been a piece of pure foolhardiness. He had told himself that he must see what was taking place, but in this he had only fooled himself; what he actually had done had been to act impulsively, and one man traveling alone must never act on impulse. And what had he found? Simply that for some unknown reason a tribe, or a combination of tribes, was holding some sort of festivity. That and the confirmation of what Wilson had written about the pyramiding of robotic brain cases.

Thinking about the brain cases, an involuntary shudder of apprehension ran through him. Even here, in the early morning light, safely hidden in a lilac clump, the memory of the brain cases could still trigger a strange residual and unreasoning fear. Why should this be so? he wondered. What about the brain cases could arouse such an emotion in a man?

A few birds were singing their morning songs. The slight breeze that had blown in the night had died with dawn and not a leaf was stirring. He finished with the jerky and put it back in the pack. He hitched himself away from the cluster of tree trunks against which he had been leaning and stretched out to sleep.

7

She was waiting for him when he crawled out of the lilac thicket in the middle of the afternoon. She stood directly in front of the tunnel he had made to force his way into the thicket, and the first indication he had that anyone was there came when he saw two bare feet planted in the grass at the tunnel's end. They were dirty feet, streaked with flaking mud, and the toenails were untrimmed and broken. He froze at the sight of them and his eyes traveled up the tattered, tarnished, grease-stained robe that reached down to her ankles. The robe ended and he saw her face—a face half hidden in a tangled mop of iron-gray hair. Beneath the mop of hair were a pair of steely eyes, now lighted with hidden laughter, the crow's-feet at the corners of them crinkled in merriment. The mouth was a thin slash and twisted, the lips close-pressed, as if trying to hold in a shout of glee. He stared up at her foolishly, his neck craned at a painful angle.

A Heritage of Stars

Seeing that he'd seen her, she cackled at him and did a shuffling jig.

"Aye, laddie, now I have you," she shouted. "I have you where I want you, crawling on your belly and kissing my feet. I had you spotted all the day and I've been waiting for you, being very careful not to disturb your beauty rest. It is shameful, it is, and you with the mark upon you."

His eyes flashed to each side of her, sick with apprehension, shamed at being trapped by an odious old hag who shouted gibberish at him. But she was alone, he saw; there was no one else about.

"Well, come on out," she told him. "Stand up and let us have a look at the magnificence of you. It's not often that Old Meg catches one like you."

He tossed the bow and quiver and the packsack out beyond the tunnel's mouth and got to his feet, confronting her.

"Now look at him," she chortled. "Is he not a handsome specimen? Shining in his buckskins with egg upon his face, account of being caught at his little tricks. And sure you thought no one was a-seeing you when you came sneaking in at dawn. Although I am not claiming that I saw you; I just felt you, that was all. Like I feel the rest of them when they come sneaking in. Although, truth to tell, you did better than the rest. You looked things over well before you went so cleverly to earth. But even then I knew the mark upon you."

"Shut up the clatter," he told her roughly. "What is this mark you speak of, and you say you felt me? Do you mean you sensed me?"

"Oh, but he's a clever one," she said. "And so well spoken, too, with a fine feeling for the proper words. 'Sensed me,' he says, and I suppose that is a better word. Until now I did not clap eyes upon you, but I knew that you were there and I knew where you went and kept track of you, sleeping there, all the

49

livelong day. Aye, you cannot fool the old girl, no matter what you do."

"The mark?" he asked. "What kind of mark? I haven't any marks."

"Why, the mark of greatness, dearie. What other could it be, a fine strapping lad like you, out on a great adventure."

Angrily, he reached down to pick up his knapsack, slung it on his shoulder.

"If you've made all the fun you want of me," he said, "I'll be on my way."

She laid a hand upon his arm. "Not so fast, my bucko. It is Meg, the hilltop witch, that you are talking with. There are ways that I can help you, if I have a mind to, and I think I have a mind to, for you're a charming lad and one with a good heart in him. I sense that you need help and I hope you're not too proud to ask it. Although among the young there's always a certain arrogance of pride. My powers may be small and there are times they are so small I wonder if in truth I really am a witch, although many people seem to think so and that's as good as being one. And since they think I am, I set high fees on my work, for if I set a small fee, they'd think me a puny witch. But for you, my lad, there'll be no fee at all, for you are poorer than a church mouse and could not pay in any case."

"That's kind of you," said Cushing. "Especially since I made no solicitation of your help."

"Now listen to the pride and arrogance of him," said Meg. "He asks himself what an old bag like myself could ever do for him. Not an old bag, sonny, but one that's middle-aged. Not as good as I once was, but not exactly feeble, either. If you should want no more than a tumble in the hay, I still could acquit myself. And there's something to be said for a young one to learn the art from someone who is older and experienced. But that, I see, is not what you had in mind."

"Not exactly," Cushing said.

"Well, then, perhaps you'd like something better than trail fare to stuff your gut. The kettle's on and you'd be doing Meg a favor to sit at table with her. If you are bound to go, it might help the journey to start with a belly that is full. And I still read that greatness in you. I would like to know more about the greatness."

"There's no greatness in me," he protested. "I'm nothing but a woods runner."

"I still think it's greatness," Meg told him. "Or a push to greatness. I know it. I sensed it immediately this morning. Something in your skull. A great excitement welling in you."

"Look," he said, desperately, "I'm a woods runner, that is all. And now, if you don't mind."

She tightened her grip upon his arm. "Now, you can't go running off. Ever since I sensed you. . . ."

"I don't understand," he said, "about this sensing of me. You mean you smelled me out. Read my mind, perhaps. People don't read minds. But, wait, perhaps they can. There was something that I read—"

"Laddie, you can read?"

"Yes, of course I can."

"Then it must be the university you are from. For there be precious few outside its walls who can scan a line. What happened, my poor precious? Did they throw you out?"

"No," he said, tightly, "they did not throw me out."

"Then, sonny, there must be more to it than I ever dreamed. Although I should have known. There was the great excitement in you. University people do not go plunging out into the world unless there are great events at stake. They huddle in their safety and are scared of shadows. . . ."

"I was a woods runner," he said, "before I went to the

university. I spent five years there and now I run the woods again. I tired of potato hoeing."

"And now," she said, "the bravado of him! He swaps the hoe for a bow and marches toward the west to defy the oncoming horde. Or is this thing you seek so great that you can ignore the sweep of conquerors?"

"The thing I seek," he said, "may be no more than a legend, empty talk whispered down the years. But what is this you say about the coming of a horde?"

"You would not know, of course. Across the river, in the university, you squat behind your walls, mumbling of the past, and take no notice of what is going on outside."

"Back in the university," he said, "we knew that there was talk of conquest, perhaps afoot already."

"More than afoot," she said. "Sweeping toward us and growing as it moves. Pointed at this city. Otherwise, why the drumming of last night?"

"The thought crossed my mind," he said. "I could not be sure, of course."

"I've been on the watch for them," said Meg. "Knowing that at the first sign of them I must be on my way. For if they should find Old Meg, they'd hang her in a tree to die. Or burn her. Or visit other great indignity and pain upon this feeble body. They have no love of witches, and my name, despite my feeble powers, is not unknown to them."

"There are the people of the city," Cushing said. "They've been your customers. Through the years you've served them well. You need only go to them. They'll offer you protection."

She spat upon the ground. "The innocence of you," she said, "is terrible to behold. They'd slip a knife between my ribs. They have no love of me. They hate me. When their fears become too great, or their greed too great, or something else too great for them to bear, they come to me, yammering for help. But they come only when there's nowhere else to go, for they seem to think there's something dirty about dealing with a witch. They fear me and because of this fear; they hate me. They hate me even when they come to me for help."

"In that case, you should have been gone long since."

"There was something told me I should stay," she said. "Even when I knew that I should go. Even when I knew I was a fool not going, I still stayed on, as if I might be waiting for something. I wondered why and now I know. Perhaps my powers are greater than I dreamed. I waited for a champion and now I have one."

"The hell you have," he said.

She thrust out her chin. "I am going with you. I don't care what you say, I am going with you."

"I'm going west," he said, "and you're not going with me."

"We'll first move to the south," she said. "I know the way to go. I'll show you the way to go. South to the river and then up the river. There we'll be safe. The horde will stick to higher ground. The river valley is hard traveling and they'll not go near it."

"I'll be traveling fast," he said, "moving in the night."

"Meg has spells," she said. "She has powers that can be used. She can sense the minds of others."

He shook his head.

"I have a horse," she told him. "No great noble steed, but a gentle animal and intelligent that can carry what we need."

"I carry what I need upon my back."

"I have against the trip a ham, a slab of bacon, flour, salt, blankets, a spyglass."

"What do you mean, 'spyglass'?"

"A double-barreled spyglass."

"Binoculars, you mean."

"From long ago," she said. "Paid as a fee by a man who was very much afraid and came to seek my help."

"Binoculars would be handy," Cushing said.

"There, you see. I would not hold you up. I am spry of foot and Andy is a fey horse. He can slip along so softly he is never noticed. And you, noble seeker of a legend, would not leave a helpless woman . . ."

He snorted. "Helpless," he said.

"So, laddie, you must see that we could be of aid to one another. You with your prowess and Old Meg with her powers—"

"No," he said.

"Let us go down to the house," she said. "There we'll find a modicum of buckwheat flour to make some cakes, a jug of sorghum, perhaps a slice of ham. While we eat, you can tell me about this thing you seek and we will lay our plans."

"I'll eat your cakes," he said, "but it will gain you nothing. You are not going with me."

8

They set out with the first light of the rising moon. Cushing took the lead, pondering how it had come about that he had agreed to let Meg come along. He had kept on saying no and she had kept on saying yes and here they were, the two of them together. Could it have been witchery? he asked himself. If that should be the case—it might be, after all—it could be all right to have her with him. If she could perform witchery on others as well as she had on him, perhaps it was all right.

Although, it *was* cumbersome, he told himself. One man could slip through the woods with no thought for anyone but himself, could keep a low profile, could travel as he willed. This was not possible with two people and a horse. Especially with the horse. He should have said, he knew, "It's all right for you to come along, but the horse must stay behind." Face to face with Andy, he'd not been able to say it. He could no more have abandoned Andy than all those years ago he could have abandoned the animals when he left the coulee.

Meg had said that Andy was a fey horse and Cushing did not know about that, but when one laid eyes upon him, it could be seen that he was a loving and a trusting horse. A humble horse, as well, with no illusions about being a noble charger. A patient animal that relied on human kindness and consideration. He was a bag of bones, but despite that, there was about him a certain air of competency.

Cushing headed southwesterly, striking for the Minnesota River valley, as Meg had said they should. The Minnesota was a small, meandering stream that wriggled like a snake between low bluffs to join the Mississippi at a little distance south of where, the night before, he had crossed the larger river. The valley was heavily wooded and would afford good cover, although following its windings would add many miles to the westward journey.

He wondered, thinking of it, where they might be going. Somewhere in the West; that was all he knew. That was all Wilson had known. But how far west and in what part of the West? On the nearby high plains, or in the foothills of the Rockies, or even in the great southwestern deserts? Blind, he told himself, so blind a seeking that when one thought of it, it seemed an errant madness. Meg, when he had told her of the Place, thought that she could recall once hearing such a legend, but she could not remember when she'd heard it or whom she'd heard it from. But she had not scoffed at it; she was too glad of a chance to flee the city to engage in any scoffing. Somewhere along the way, perhaps, they'd be able to pick up further word of it. As they went west there might be someone they'd encounter who had further word of it. That is, if there were any word at all; if, in fact, there were a Place of Going to the Stars.

And if there were such a place, once they got there, what would be the profit or significance? Even if they found the place and found evidence that man at one time had flown to the stars, what would this knowledge change? Would the nomads stop their raiding and their pillaging? Would the city tribes establish the nucleus of a decent government? Would men come trooping into the university to create a renaissance that would lift mankind out of the bestial abyss into which it had been plunged?

None of these things, he knew, would happen. There'd be left only the satisfaction of knowing that at one time, more than a thousand years before, men had left the solar system and gone into the cosmos. There might be pride in that, of course, but pride alone was poor coin in the sort of place the world had now become.

And yet, he told himself, there could be no turning back. He'd set out upon a quest, perhaps impulsively, guided by emotion rather than by reason, and profitless as it might be, he must somehow keep the faith. Even if the faith be foolish, it somehow must be kept. He tried to reason why this should be and he found no answer.

By now the moon had risen well into the eastern sky. The city was behind them and they were deep into the suburbs. Off to the right a one-time water tower sagged out of the perpendicular; in a few more years it would come crashing down.

Cushing halted and waited for the others to come up. Andy bumped his muzzle in a gentle greeting against his chest, blowing softly through his nostrils. Cushing rubbed the furred head gently, pulling at the ears.

"He likes you," said Meg, "and it's not everyone he likes. He is a discerning horse. But there's no reason why he shouldn't like you, for he, as well as I, reads the mark upon you."

"Let's forget this business," Cushing said, "of a mark upon me. For I haven't any mark. What do you know of this country?

Should we keep on as we're going, or should we move toward the south?"

"To the south," she said. "The quicker we get into the valley, the safer we will be."

"This horde you were telling me about—how far off are they?"

"A day or two, mayhaps. City scouts a week ago sighted them a hundred miles to the west, pulling their forces together and about to move. It is most likely they'll move at an easy pace, for in their minds there can seem no hurry. The city lies there for their easy picking and they would have no way of knowing that they had been spotted."

"And they'll be coming straight in from the west?"

"Laddie boy, I do not know, but that is what I think."

"So we do have a little time?"

"The margin is close enough," she warned him. "There is no sense in the cutting of it finer. We can breathe the easier once we reach the valley."

Cushing moved off again and the two fell in behind him.

The land was empty. An occasional rabbit popped out of cover and went leaping in the moonlight. At times, a disturbed bird would twitter sleepily. Once, from down in the river valley, they heard the whicker of a coon.

Behind Cushing, Andy snorted suddenly. Cushing came to a stop. The horse had heard or seen something and it would be wise to heed his warning.

Meg came up softly. "What is it, laddie boy?" she asked.

"Andy sensed something. Do you see anything?"

"Don't move," he said. "Get down, close against the ground. Keep quiet. Don't move."

There seemed to be nothing. Mounds that once had been houses. Thickets of shrubs. The long lines of old boulevard trees.

Behind him, Andy made no further sound.

Directly ahead of them, planted in the center of what once had been a street, a boulder squatted. Not too big a boulder, reaching perhaps as high as a man's waist. Funny that there should be a boulder in the middle of a street.

Meg, crouching close against the ground, reached out to touch his leg. She whispered at him. "There is someone out there. I can sense them. Faint, far off."

"How far?"

"I don't know. Far and weak."

"Where?"

"Straight ahead of us."

They waited. Andy stamped a foot and then was quiet.

"It's frightening," said Meg. "Cold shivers. Not like us."

"Us?"

"Humans. Not like humans."

In the river valley the coon whickered once again. Cushing's eyes ached as he concentrated on seeing the slightest motion, the faintest sign.

Meg whispered, "It's the boulder."

"Someone hiding behind it," Cushing said.

"No one hiding. It's the boulder. Different."

They waited.

"Funny place for that rock to be," said Cushing. "In the middle of the street. Who would have moved it there? Why would they have moved it there?"

"The rock's alive," said Meg. "It could have moved itself."

"Rocks don't move," he said. "Someone has to move them."

She said nothing.

"Stay here," he said.

He dropped the bow, pulled the hatchet from his belt, then ran swiftly forward. He stopped just short of the boulder. Nothing happened. He ran forward again, swung around the boulder. There was nothing behind it. He put out a hand and touched it. It was warm, warmer than it should have been. The sun had been down for hours and by now the rock should have lost all the solar radiation that it had picked up during the day, but it was still faintly warm. Warm and smooth, slippery to the touch. As if someone had polished it.

Andy shuffled forward, Meg walking with him.

"It's warm," said Cushing.

"It's alive," said Meg. "Write that one down, my bucko. It's a living stone. Or it's not a stone, but something that looks like one."

"I don't like it," said Cushing. "It smells of witchery."

"No witchery," said Meg. "Something else entirely. Something very dreadful. Something that should never be. Not like a man, not like anything at all. Frozen memories. That is what I sense. Frozen memories, so old that they are frozen. But there is no telling what they are. An uncaring, maybe. A cold uncaring."

Cushing looked around. All was peaceful. The trees were etched against the sky in the whiteness of the moonlight. The sky was soft and there were many stars. He tried to fight down the terror that he felt rising in him, like a bitter gall gushing in his throat.

"You ever hear of anything like this before?" he asked.

"No, never, laddie. Never in my life."

"Let's get out of here," he said.

9

A great wind sweeping across the valley at some time earlier in the year had cut a narrow swath through the trees that grew between the river's bank and the blufftop. Great monarchs of the forest lay in a giant hedge, twisted and uprooted. Shriveled, drying leaves still clung to many of the branches.

"We'll be safe here," said Cushing. "Anyone coming from the west, even if they wanted to come down to the river, would have to swing around these trees."

By holding branches to one side so he could get through, they cleared the way for Andy to work his way through the tangle into a small clear area where there would be room for him to lie down and enough grass for him to make a meal.

Cushing pointed to a den formed by the uprooting of a huge black oak, the rooted stump canted at an angle, overhanging the cavity gouged out of the earth by its uprooting.

"In there," he said, "we won't be seen if anyone comes nosing around."

Meg said, "I'll cook breakfast for you, laddie. What do you want? Hot bread and bacon, maybe?"

"Not yet," he said. "Not now. We have to be careful with a fire. Nothing but the driest wood, so there'll be no smoke, and not too big a fire. I'll take care of it after I get back. Don't try it yourself. I want to be sure about the fire. Someone gets a whiff of smoke and they'll start looking."

"After you get back. Where you be going, sonny?"

"Up on the bluff," he said. "I want to have a look. See if there's anyone about."

"Take the spyglass with you, then."

Atop the bluff, he looked across a stretch of rolling prairie, with only occasional clumps of trees. Far to the north was what once had been a group of farm buildings, standing in a small grove. Of the buildings there was little left. Through the glasses he could make out what once had been a barn, apparently a sturdily built structure. Part of the roof had collapsed, but otherwise it still stood. Beyond it was a slight mound that probably marked the site of another, less substantial building. Part of a pole fence still existed, raggedly running nowhere.

Squatting in a clump of brush that would serve to break up his outline if anyone should be watching, he patiently and methodically glassed the prairie, taking his time, working from the west to the east.

A small herd of deer were feeding on the eastern side of a small knoll. He caught a badger sitting at its burrow's mouth. A red fox sat on a stone that jutted from a low hillside, watching the countryside for any game that might be picked up easily.

Cushing kept on watching. There must be no sloppiness, he told himself; he needed to be sure there was nothing but the animals. He started in the west again and moved slowly eastward. The deer were still there, but the badger had disappeared. More than likely it had popped into its den. The fox was gone, as well.

To one side he caught a sense of motion. Swiveling the glasses smoothly, he caught the motion in the field. It was far off, but seemed to be moving fast. As it came nearer, he saw what it was: a body of horsemen. He tried to count them, but they were still too far away. They were not, he saw, coming directly toward him, but angling to the southeast. He watched in fascination. Finally he could count them. Either nineteen or twenty; he could not be absolutely sure. They were dressed in furs and leathers, and carried shields and spears. Their little, short-coupled horses moved at a steady lope.

So Meg had been right. The horde was on the move. The band out of the prairie were perhaps no more than outflankers for the main force, which probably was to the north.

He watched until they had moved out of sight, then searched the prairie again for other possible bands. None showed up, and satisfied, finally, he replaced the glasses in the case and moved off the hill and down the bluff. There might be other small bands, he knew, but there was no point in waiting for them. Meg was probably right: they'd stay out on the prairie, headed for the city and away from the river valley.

Halfway down the bluffside a voice spoke to him from the tangle of fallen trees.

"Friend," it said. Not a loud voice, but clearly spoken, pitched to reach his ear.

At the sound, he froze his stride, glanced swiftly about.

"Friend," the voice spoke again, "could you find it in your heart to succor a most unfortunate?"

A trick? Cushing wondered. He reached swiftly over his shoulder for an arrow from the quiver.

"There is no need to fear," the voice spoke again. "Even had

I the wish, I am in no position to bring you any harm. I am hard pinned beneath a tree and I would be grateful for any help that you could render me."

Cushing hesitated. "Where are you?" he asked.

"To your right," the voice said. "At the edge of the fallen trees. I can see you from where I lie. Should you hunker down, you undoubtedly could glimpse me."

Cushing put the arrow aside and hunkered down, squinting into the maze of fallen branches. A face stared out at him and at the sight of it he sucked in his breath in astonishment. Such a face he had never seen before. A skull-like face, fashioned of hard planes that shone in the sunlight that filtered through the branches.

"Who are you?" he asked.

"I am Rollo, the robot."

"Rollo? A robot? You can't be a robot. There are no longer any robots."

"There is I," said Rollo. "I would not be surprised if I were the last of them."

"But if you're a robot, what are you doing here?"

"I told you, remember? I am pinned beneath a tree. A small tree, luckily, but still impossible to escape from it. My leg is caught, and free I've tried to pull it, but that's impossible. I have tried to dig the soil to release my leg by which I'm trapped, but that is impossible as well. Beneath the leg lies a ledge or rock; upon it lies the tree. I cannot squirm around to lift the tree. I've tried everything and there is nothing I can do."

Cushing bent over and ducked beneath the overhanging branches. Squirming forward, he reached the fallen robot and squatted on his heels to look at the situation.

There had been imaginative drawings of robots, he recalled, in some of the magazines he'd found in the library—robots that had been drawn before there were any actual robots. The drawings had represented great, ungainly metal men who undoubtedly would have done a lot of clanking when they walked. Rollo was nothing like them. He was a slender creature, almost spindly. His shoulders were broad and heavy and his head atop the shoulders seemed a bit too large, somewhat out of proportion, but the rest of him tapered down to a narrow waist, with a slight broadening of the hips to accommodate the sockets of the legs. The legs were trim and neat; looking at them, Cushing thought of the trim legs of a deer. One of the legs, he saw, was pinned beneath a heavy branch that had split off the mighty maple when it had struck the ground. The branch was somewhat more than a foot in diameter.

Rollo saw Cushing looking at the branch. "I could have lifted it enough to pull my leg out," he said, "but there was no way I could twist around to get a good grip on it."

"Let's see what I can do," said Cushing.

He moved forward on hands and knees, got his hands beneath the branch. He hefted it gingerly, found he could barely move it.

"Maybe I can lift it enough," he said. "I'll let you know when I'm ready to lift. Then you try to pull the leg out."

Cushing crept closer, settling his knees solidly under him, bent and got both arms around the branch.

"Now," he said. Straining, he heaved up, felt the branch move slightly, heaved again.

"I'm out," said Rollo. "You didn't have to move it much."

Carefully, Cushing slid his arms free, let the branch drop back into place.

Rollo was crawling around on the ground. He retrieved a leather bag from where it lay beneath a pile of leaves, scrabbled around some more and came up with an iron-tipped spear.

"I couldn't reach them before," he said. "When the branch fell on me, they flew out of my hands."

"You all right?" asked Cushing.

"Sure, I'm all right," the robot said. He sat up, hoisted the formerly trapped foot into his lap and examined it.

"Not even dented," he said. "The metal's tough."

"Would you mind telling me how you got into this mess?"

"Not at all," said Rollo. "I was walking along when a storm came up. I wasn't worried much. A little rain won't hurt me. Then the tornado hit. I heard it coming and I tried to run. I guess what I did was run right into it. There were trees crashing all around me. The wind started to lift me, then set me down again. When I came down, I fell, sort of sprawled out. That's when I was pinned. The limb broke off and caught me. Then it was all over. The storm passed on, but I couldn't move. I thought at first it was just a small inconvenience. I was confident I could work free. But, as you see, there was no way of working free."

"How long ago did all this happen?"

"I can tell you that exactly. I kept count. Eighty-seven days. The thing I was worried about was rust. I had some bear oil in my bag. . . ."

"Bear oil?"

"Sure, bear oil. First you kill a bear, then build a fire and render out his fat. Any fat will do, but bear oil is the best. Where else would you get oil except from animals? Once we used a petro-product, but there's not been any of that for centuries. Animal fat isn't good, but it serves its purpose. You have to take care of a body such as mine. You can allow no rust to get a start. The metal's fairly good, but even so, rust can get a start. The eighty-seven days were no great problem, but if you hadn't come along, I'd have been in trouble. I had it figured out that in time the wood would rot and then I could work free. But that might have taken several years. I don't know how many.

"It was a little boresome, too. The same things to look at all the time. Nothing to talk with. I had this Shivering Snake that hung around for years. Never doing anything, of course, of no use whatever, but always skittering around and sneaking up on you and then sort of backing off, as if it were playing games with you, or whatnot. But when I got pinned underneath that tree, Old Shivering disappeared and I haven't seen it since. If it'd stuck around, it would have been some sort of company, something at least to watch, and I could talk to it. It never answered back, of course, but I talked to it a lot. It was something one could talk to. But once I got pinned underneath that tree, it lit out, and I haven't seen it since."

"Would you mind telling me," said Cushing, "just what is a Shivering Snake?"

"I don't know," said Rollo. "It was the only one I ever saw. I never heard of anyone ever seeing one before. Never even heard any talk of one. It was really not much of anything at all. Just a shimmer. It didn't walk or run, just shivered in the air, sparkling all the time. In the sunlight you couldn't see it sparkle very well, but in the dark it was spectacular. Not any kind of shape. No shape at all, I guess, or anything at all. Just a blob of sparkling, dancing in the air."

"You have no idea what it was or where it came from? Or why it hung out with you?"

"At times I thought it was a friend of mine," said Rollo, "and I was glad of that, for I tell you, mister, as possibly the last robot, I'm not exactly up to my hips in friends. Most people, if they saw me, would think of me as no more than an opportunity to collect another brain case. You don't happen to have any designs on my brain case, do you?"

"None at all," said Cushing.

"That is good," said Rollo, "because if you had, I'd have to warn you that if forced to, I would kill you to protect myself. Robots, in case you didn't know, were inhibited against killing anything at all, against any kind of violence. It was implanted in us. That's why there aren't any robots left. They allowed themselves to be run down and killed without the lifting of a hand to protect themselves. Either that or they hid out and caught the rust. Even when they could get hold of some lubricant to keep away the rust, the supply didn't last forever, and when it was gone, they could get no more. So they rusted and that was the end of them, except for the brain case, which could not rust. And after many years, someone came along and found the brain case and collected it.

"Well, after my small supply of lubricant ran out, I took counsel with myself and I told myself this silliness of a robot being so disgustingly nonviolent might have been all right under the old order, but under this new order that had come along, it made no sense at all. I figured there was oil to be got from animal fat if I could only bring myself to kill. Faced with extinction, I decided I would break the inhibition and would kill for fat, and I worked it out that a bear was the thing to kill, for ordinarily, bear are loaded with fat. But it was no easy thing to do, I tell you. I rigged me up a spear and practiced with it until I knew how to handle it, then set out to kill a bear. As you might guess, I failed. I just couldn't do it. I'd get all set and then I'd go all soft inside. Maybe I never would have worked up my courage on my own. By this time I was considerably discouraged. There were a few rust spots beginning to show up and I knew that was the beginning of the end. I had about given up when one day, out somewhere in the mountains, a big grizzly caught sight of me. I don't know what was the matter with him. He was short-tempered and there must have been something that had happened to shorten up his temper. I've often wondered what it was. Maybe he had a toothache, or a thorn in his foot. I will never know. Maybe the sight of me reminded him of something that he didn't like. But anyhow, first thing that I know, here he is barreling down upon me, with his shoulders humping and his mouth wide open, roaring, and those big claws reaching out. I suppose that if I'd had the time, I would have turned and run. But I didn't have the time and I didn't have the space to run. But the way it was, when he was almost on top of me, the fright that I had felt suddenly turned to anger. Maybe desperation more than anger, really, and I thought, in that instant before he closed on me, you son of a bitch, maybe you can mangle and disable me, but in doing it, I'm going to mangle and disable you. And I remember this distinctly, the one thing I do remember well out of all of it—just before he reached me, with this new anger in me, I brought up my spear and jumped at him even as he lunged at me. After this, there is not much that I do remember. It was all a haze and a blur. When my mind came clear again, I was standing on my feet, covered with blood, with a bloody knife in hand, and the bear stretched out on the ground, with my spear buried in his throat.

"That did it. That snapped the inhibition. Killing once, I could kill again. I rendered the fat of this old grizzly and I found a sandy creek. For days I camped beside the creek, using sand to scrape off the few rust spots that had developed on me and keeping myself well greased. Ever since I've kept well greased. I never run out of grease. There are a lot of bear.

"But I have been running on so that I haven't asked you who you are. That is, if you want to tell me. A lot of people would just as soon not tell you who they are. But you come along and rescue me and I don't know who you are. I don't know who to thank."

"I'm Tom Cushing. And there need not be any thanks. Let's

get out of here. I have a camp just a step away. Have you got all your things?"

"Just the bag and spear. That was all I had. I had a knife and it's still in the sheath."

"Now that you are free," said Cushing. "what plans do you have?"

"Why, no plans at all," said Rollo. "I never have a plan. I simply wander. I have wandered with no purpose for more years than I can count. At one time it troubled me—this lack of purpose. But it does no longer. Although I suppose that if I were offered a purpose, I would gratefully accept it. Does it happen, friend, that you may have a purpose you would share with me? For I do owe you something."

"You owe me nothing," Cushing said, "but I do have a purpose. We can talk about it."

10

The Trees ringed the great butte, having watched through the night as they had watched through centuries, through cold and heat, wet and dry, noon and midnight, cloud and sun. Now the sun came up over the eastern horizon and as its warmth and light fell on them, they greeted it with all the holy ecstacy and thankfulness they had felt when it first had fallen on them, as new-planted saplings put out to serve the purpose they had served through the years, their sensitivity and emotion undimmed by time.

They took the warmth and light and sucked it in and used it. They knew the movement of the dawn breeze and rejoiced in it, fluttering their leaves in response to it. They adjusted themselves to take and use the heat, monitored the limited amount of water that their roots could reach, conserving it, taking up in their roots only what they needed, for this was dryland and water must be used most wisely. And they watched; they continued watching. They noted all that happened. They knew the fox that skulked back to its den with the coming of dawn; the owl that flew back home, half blinded by the morning light (it had stayed out too long) to the small grove of cottonwoods that lined the tiny stream where water flowed begrudgingly along a rocky course; the mice that, having escaped the fox and owl, ran squealing in their grassy burrows; the lumbering grizzly that humped across the desiccated plain, the great lord of the land that brooked no interference from anything alive, including those strange, two-legged, upright creatures the Trees glimpsed occasionally; the distant herd of wild cattle that grazed on scanty pasturage, ready to gallop in a calculated frenzy should the lumbering bear head in their direction; the great bird of prey that sailed high the air, viewing the vast territory that was its own, hungry now, but confident that before the day was out it would find the dead or dying that would give it meat.

The Trees knew the structure of the snowflake, the chemistry of the raindrop, the molecular pattern of the wind. They realized the fellowship of grasses, of other trees and bushes, the springtime brilliance of the prairie flowers that bloomed briefly in their season; had friendship for the birds that nested in their branches; were aware of ant and bee and butterfly.

They gloried in the sun and knew all that went on around them and talked with one another, not so much a matter of relaying information (although they could do that if need be) as a matter of acknowledging one another's presence, of making themselves known, of saying all was well—a time of comradely contact to know that all was well.

Above them, on the butte, the ancient buildings stood high against the skyline, against the paleness of the blue that held no single cloud, a sky burnished by the rising sun and scrubbed clean by the summer

11

The small fire burned with no smoke. Meg knelt beside it to cook the pan of bread. Off to one side, Rollo sat absorbed in the ritual of greasing himself, pouring ill-smelling bear oil out of a bottle fashioned from a gourd. Andy stamped and swished his tail to keep away the flies while paying serious attention to the spotty clumps of grass that were scattered here and there. A short distance away the unseen river gurgled and chuckled as it surged between its banks. The sun was halfway up the eastern sky and the day would get warmer later on, but here, in their hiding place beneath the fallen trees, the temperature was still pleasant.

"You say, laddie," said Meg, "that the band you sighted numbered only twenty?"

"Thereabouts," said Cushing. "I could not be sure. No more than that, I think."

"A scout party, more than likely. Sent out, no doubt, to probe the city. To spot the locations of the tribes. Mayhaps we should stay here for a while. This is a snug retreat and not easily found."

Cushing shook his head. "No, we'll push on, come night. If the horde is moving east and we are going west, we should soon be free of them."

She inclined her head toward the robot. "And what of him?" she asked.

"If he wishes, he can go with us. I've not talked with him about it."

"I sense about this enterprise," said Rollo, "a seeming urgency and purpose. Even not knowing what it is, I would be willing for the chance to associate myself with it. I pride myself that I might be of some small service. Not needing sleep myself, I could keep a watch while others slept. Being sharp of eye and swift of movement, I could do some scouting. I am well acquainted with the wilds, since I have been forced to live in them, well beyond the haunts of men. I would consume no supplies, since I live on solar energy alone. Give me a few days' sunshine and I have energy stored against a month or more. And I am a good companion, for I never tire of talk."

"That is right," said Cushing. "He has not stopped talking since the minute I found him."

"Reduced, at many times, I've been," said Rollo, "to talking to myself. Which is not bad if there is no one else to talk with. Talking with oneself, it's possible to find many areas of precise agreement, and one need never talk on subjects that are not agreeable.

"The best year I ever spent was long ago when, in the depths of the Rockies, I chanced upon an old mountain man who stood in need of help. He was an ancient personage who had fallen victim to a strange disease of stiffening muscles and aching joints, and had it not been for my coming accidentally upon him, he would not have lasted out the winter, since when the cold came he would not have been capable of hunting meat or bringing in the wood that was needed to keep his cabin warm. I stayed with him and brought in game and wood, and since he was as starved for talk as I was, we talked away the winter, he telling of great events in which he had participated or to which he had been a witness, and in many of them there may have been something less than truth, although I never questioned them, for so far as I was concerned, talk, not truth, was paramount. And I spinning tales for him, but little ornamented, of the days I'd spent since the Time of Trouble. Early the next summer, when the pain in him was less and he was able to make his way about, he set off for what he called a "rendezvous," a summer place of meeting for others such as he. He asked me to go with him, but I declined, for truth to tell, I no longer have any love of man. Excepting the present company, which seems well intentioned, I have had nothing except trouble in those few times I have blundered into men."

"You can remember the Time of Trouble, then?" said Cushing. "You have lived through it all, and your memory's clear?"

"Oh, clear enough," said Rollo. "I recall the things that happened, but it would be bootless for you to ask me the meaning of it, for I had no understanding of it then, and despite much thinking on it, have no understanding of it now. You see, I was a common yard robot, a runner of errands and a performer of chores. I had no training except in simple tasks, although I understand there were many of my kind who did have some special training, who were skilled technicians and many other things. My memories mostly are unpleasant, although in recent centuries I have learned to live with existing situations, taking each day as it comes and not ranting against conditions as they are. I was not designed to be a lonely mechanism, but that is what I have been forced to become. I have, through bitter circumstances, become able to live for and of myself, although I am never really happy of it. That is why I have so willingly suggested that I associate myself with your enterprise."

"Not even knowing," Meg asked, "what the enterprise might be?"

"Even so," said Rollo, "if it so happens later on that I do not like the look or smell of it, I can simply walk away."

"It's no evil enterprise," said Cushing. "It's a simple search. We are looking for a Place of Going to the Stars."

Rollo nodded sagely. "I have heard of it. Not extensively. Nothing that is greatly known, but of which one hears occasionally, many years apart. It is situated, as best I can determine, on a mesa or a butte somewhere in the West. The mesa or the butte is ringed in by an extensive growth of Trees that legend says keep watch upon the place and will allow no one to enter. And there are other devices, it is said, that guard it, although of those devices I have no true and certain knowledge."

"Then there is such a place?"

Rollo spread his hands. "Who knows. There are many tales of strange places, strange things, strange people. The old man I spent the winter with mentioned it—I think only once. But he told many stories and not all of them were truth. He said the place was called Thunder Butte."

"Thunder Butte," said Cushing. "Would you know where Thunder Butte might be?"

Rollo shook his head. "Somewhere in the Great Plains country. That is all I know. Somewhere beyond the great Missouri."

12

Excerpt from Wilson's *History*:

One of the strange evolutions which seems to have followed the Collapse and which has developed in the centuries since is the rise of special human faculties and abilities. There are many stories of certain personalities who possess these abilities, some of them surpassing all belief, although as to the truth of them, there is none to say.

On the shelves at this university is an extensive literature on the possibilities of the paranormal and, in fact, some case histories that would appear to indicate the realization of such possibilities. It is only fair to point out, however, that a great part of this literature is theoretical and in some instances controversial. On a close examination of the pre-Collapse literature (which is all we have, of course), it would appear reasonable to conclude that there are enough convincing instances reported of the psychic or the paranormal to lend some substance to a belief that some of the theories may be correct.

Since the Collapse, although there has been no documentation upon which a judgment can be founded, it appears that a greater concentration of paranormal and psychic phenomena has been observed than was the case before. One must realize, certainly, that none of these reports can be subjected to the kind of critical examination and survey as was possible in the past. For this reason, that none of them is weeded out, they may appear to be more frequent than they really are. Each instance, once it is reported, becomes a story to be told in wondering amazement and with no great concern as to whether it be true or not. But even taking all this into account, the impression still holds that this type of phenomenon is, indeed, increasing.

There are those at this university, with whom I've talked, who feel that this increase may be due, in part at least, to the lifting and the shattering of the physically scientific and technological mold which prior to the Collapse encased all humanity. If a man (or a woman), these colleagues of mine point out, is told often enough that something is impossible, or worse, is foolishness, then there is a lessening of the willingness to believe in it, or to subscribe to it. This might mean that those pre-Collapse people who had a bent toward the psychic or the paranormal may have squelched their own abilities or (much to the same point) any dedicated belief in their abilities (for who would fly in the face of impossibility or engage in foolish practices?), with the result that any progress in the field was thwarted. The end result would be that an entire field of human endeavors and abilities may have been sidetracked, if not eliminated, in the face of the technologically minded dictum that they were either foolish or impossible.

Today no such dictum remains. Technological thinking was at least discredited, if not entirely wiped out, with the destruc-

tion of the machines and the social systems they had built. Which, after a century or two, left the human race free to carry out that foolishness which before had been frowned upon, if not, indeed, proscribed, by a technological mentality. It may be, too, that the present situation created a climate and environment in which nontechnological thinking and approaches to human problems have a chance to thrive. One wonders, thinking of it, what the world might have been if the science that man had subscribed to had not been almost exclusively a physical and a biological science and if, in such a case, technology had not come about. The best situation, of course, would have been if all sciences and the ideas deriving from them had been allowed equality, so that all could work together and interact. The way it turned out, however, was that the arrogance of one way of thought served to strangle all other ways of thought. . . .

13

They traveled up the river, moving in daylight now since there were two of them to watch the prairie—either Cushing or Rollo scouting the blufftops, on lookout for war parties or for other dangers. In the first few days they spotted several bands; none of these were interested in the river valley, but were moving eastward. Watching them, Cushing felt a pang of worry about the university, but told himself it was unlikely it would be attacked. Even if it were, its high wall would hold off any attacker except one that would be more persistent than a nomad band.

The Minnesota River, up which they moved, was a more placid stream than the Mississippi. It meandered through its wooded valley as a lazy man might walk, not exactly loitering, but in no hurry either. By and large it was a narrow stream, although at times it spread out through low-lying marshes and they were forced to make their way around.

To begin with, Cushing fretted at the slow time they were

making. Alone he could have covered twice the ground in half the time, but as the days went on and no more war bands appeared, the urgency fell away. After all, he realized, there was no time limit imposed upon the journey.

Having shed his fretfulness, he settled down to enjoying the trip. During the years at the university, he somehow had forgotten the exhilaration of the free life that he now followed once again: the early, foggy chill of mornings; the climb of the sun up the eastern sky; the sound of wind among the leaves; the V-shaped wake traced by a swimming muskrat; the sudden beauty of a hidden patch of flowers; the hooting of the owls once dusk settled on the river; the whicker of raccoons; the howling of the blufftop wolves. They lived high on the hog: fish from the river, squirrel and dumplings, plump fried rabbit, an occasional partridge or duck.

"This is better eating, laddie boy," said Meg, "than chewing on that chunk of jerky you carry in your knapsack."

He growled at her. "There may come a time," he said, "when we'll be glad to have the jerky."

For this was the trip's easy part, he knew, the fat time. When they had to leave the river valley and strike west across the plains, they would face hard going.

After a few days Rollo's Shivering Snake came back again and danced around him. It was an elusive and ridiculous thing, a tiny pinch of stardust shimmering in the sunlight, shining with a strange light of its own in the darkness of the night.

"Once I thought it was a friend of mine," said Rollo. "A strange thing, you might say, to look upon a little shimmer of light as a friend, but to one who has been alone and friendless over many centuries, even such an unsubstantial thing as a sparkle in the sunshine can seem to be a friend. I came to find, however, that it was a fair-weather friend. When I was pinned beneath the tree, it deserted me and did not come back till now. During all those days, I could have used it; had it been there, I could have told myself that I was not alone. Don't ask me what it is, for I have no idea. I have spent many hours puzzling out some sort of rationalization so I could put an explanation to it. But I never found one. And don't ask me when it first attached itself to me, for the time runs back so far that I would be tempted to say it was always with me. Although that would not be right, for I can recall the time when it was not with me."

The robot talked incessantly. He ran on and on, as if all the years of loneliness had dammed up a flood of words that must now come out.

"I can recall what you term the Time of Trouble," he told them, sitting around the meager campfire (meager and well hidden, so it would not show too great a light), "but I can throw no great understanding on it, for I was in no position to know what the situation might have been. I was a yard robot at a great house that stood high on a hill above a mighty river, although it was not this river you call the Mississippi, but another river somewhere in the East. I'm not sure I ever knew the river's name nor the name of those who owned the house, for there were things a yard robot would not have been required to know, so would not have been told. But after a time, perhaps some time after it all started, although I can't be sure, the word came to me and other robots that people were smashing machines. This we could not understand. After all, we did know that everyone placed great reliance on machines. I recall that we talked about it and speculated on it and we found no answers. I don't think we expected any answers. By this time the people who lived in the house had fled; why they fled or where they might have gone we had no way of knowing. No one, you must understand, ever told us anything. We were told what to do and that was all we ever needed to know. We continued to do our familiar and accustomed tasks, although now there was no one to tell us what to do, and whether we did our tasks or not did not really matter.

"Then one day—I recall this well, for it came as a shock to me—one of the robots told us that after some thought upon the matter he had come to the conclusion that we were machines as well, that if the wrecking of machines continued, we, in our turn, also would be wrecked. The wreckers, he said, had not turned to us as yet because we were of less importance than the other machines that were being wrecked. But our time would come, he said, when they got through with the others. This, as you can imagine, caused great consternation among us and no small amount of argument. There were those among us who could immediately perceive that we were, indeed, machines, while there were fully as many others who were convinced that we were not. I remember that I listened to the arguments for a time, taking no great part in them, but, finally taking private counsel with myself, came to the conclusion that we were machines, or at least could be classified as machines. And coming to this conclusion, I wasted no time in lamentation but fell to thinking, If this should be the case, what course could I take to protect myself? Finally it seemed clear to me that the best course would be to find a place where the wreckers would not think to look for me. I did not urge this course upon my fellows—for who was I to tell them what to do?—and I think I realized that one robot, acting on his own, might have a better chance of escaping the wrath that might come upon us if he were not with the other robots, since a band of us might attract attention while a single robot had a better chance of escaping all detection.

"So I left as quietly as I could and hid in many places, for there was no one safe place to hide. Finally, I gained confirmation from other fugitive robots I met that the wreckers, having smashed the more important machines, were hunting down the robots. And not, mind you, because we posed any great threat to them, but because we were machines and the idea seemed to be to wipe out all machines, no matter how insignificant. What made it even worse was that they did not hunt us down in the same spirit, in the rage and fanaticism, that had driven them to destroy the other machines, but were hunting us as a sport, as they might hunt a fox or coon. If this had not been so, we could have stood the hunting better, for then we would at least have been accorded the dignity of posing a threat to them. But there was no dignity in being hunted as a dog might run down a rabbit. To add further indignity, I learned that when we were run down and disabled, our brain cases were seized as trophies of the hunt. This, I think, was the final thing that heaped up the bitterness and fear that came to infuse us all. The terrible thing about it was that all we could do was run or hide, for we were inhibited against any kind of violence. We could not protect ourselves; we could only run. In my own case, I broke that inhibition, much later and more through accident than otherwise. If that half-mad grizzly had not attacked me, I'd still be saddled by the inhibition. Which is not quite right, either, for if he'd not attacked me to break the inhibition, I never would have been able to obtain the grease I use to protect myself from rust and would be, by now, a rusted hulk with my brain case waiting for someone to find and take home as a souvenir."

"Not exactly as a souvenir," said Cushing. "There is more to it than that. Attached to the brain cases of your fellows is a mystic symbolism that is not understood. A thousand years ago a man at the university wrote a history of the Time of Trouble and, in the course of his writing, speculated upon the ritual of the brain-case collections and their symbolism, but without reaching a conclusion. Until I read his history, I had not heard of the custom. I spent three years of woods-running, mainly in the South, and I had never heard of it. Perhaps it was because I made it my business to stay away from people. That's a good rule for a lone woods runner to follow. I walked around the tribes. Except by accident, I stayed away from everyone."

Rollo reached for his bag and dug around in it. "I carry here," he said, "the brain case of an unknown comrade. I have carried it for years. As a matter of sentiment, perhaps; perhaps as a loyalty; perhaps as a defender and caretaker of the dead; I do not know. I found it many years ago in an old deserted settlement, a former town. I saw it gleaming in the sun, not all of it, just a part of it that was exposed. It lay in a bed of rust that once had been a robotic head and skull. Digging further, I found the outline of the body, gone to rust, no more than a discoloration in the soil. That is what happened to the most of us, perhaps all of us, except myself, who escaped the human hunters. Once we no longer had any kind of oil to protect our bodies, the rust would set in and over the years would gradually spread, like a disease over which we had no control, biting ever more deeply into us until the day came when it disabled us and we could no longer move. We would lie where we had fallen, crippled by the rust, and as the years went by, the rust would burrow ever deeper. Finally, we would be a heap of rust, a pattern of rust that showed the outlines of the body. The leaves would drift over the outline, and forest mold or prairie mold, formed either by rotting leaves or rotting grasses, would cover us and hide us. The wind would sprinkle other dust over us and plants would grow in us or on top of us, more luxuriantly than elsewhere, feeding on the iron that once had been our bodies. But the brain case, built of some indestructible metal which today we cannot put a name to, would remain. So I took this brain case and put it in my sack, to cheat the human who might come along and find it. Better for me to have it and to guard it, than for some human—"

"You hate humans?" Meg asked.

"No, I never hated them. Feared them, yes; I feared them. I kept out of their way. But there have been some I have not feared. The old hunter that I spent almost a year with. And the two of you. You saved me from the tree."

He handed over the brain case. "Here," he said, "have a look at it. Have you ever seen one?"

"No, I never have," said Meg.

She sat, turning it over and over, with the firelight glinting redly on it. Finally she handed it back and Rollo put it in the sack.

The next morning, when Rollo had gone out to scout, she spoke to Cushing.

"That brain case, laddie. The one the robot let me look at. It's alive. I could sense it. I could feel the aliveness of it through my fingertips. It was cold, but alive and sharp and dark—so dark, so alone, and yet, in some ways, not alone. No expectations and yet not without hope. As if the coldness and the darkness were a way of life. And alive. I know it was alive."

Cushing drew in his breath sharply. "That means—"

"You are right. If this one is alive, so are all the others of them. All those that have been collected. All those that lie in unsuspected places."

"Without any external sensory perceptions," said Cushing. "Cut off from all sight, all sound, contact with any other life. A man would go crazy. . . ."

"A man, yes. These things are not men, my bucko. They are a cry from another time. Robots—we speak the word, of course, but we do not know what they were, or are. Robot brain cases, we say, but no one, no one except the two of us, suspects they are still alive. Robots, we thought, were extinct.

They had an old-time legendary ring, like dragons. Then one day you came walking into camp with a robot tagging you. Tell me, did you ask him to stay with us? Or did he ask to stay?"

"Neither one. He just stayed. Like he stayed a year or so with the old hunter. But I'm glad to have him. He is a lot of help. I don't think you should tell him what you just now told me."

"Never," said Meg. "No, he'd take it hard. It would haunt him. It's better if he thinks of them as dead."

"Maybe he knows."

"I don't think so," she said.

She made a cupping motion with her hand, as if she still held the brain case.

"Laddie," she said, "I could weep for them. For all the poor lost things shut up inside the darkness. But the thought occurs to me they may not need my tears. They may have something else."

"Stability," said Cushing. "Enduring a condition that would drive a man insane. Perhaps a strange philosophy that discovers within themselves some factor that makes it unnecessary to have external contact. You made no effort to communicate, to reach out to them?"

"I could not have been so cruel," said Meg. "I wanted to; the urge was there. To let it know it was not alone, to give it some sort of comfort. And then I realized how cruel that would have been. To give it hope when there is no hope. To disturb it after it had spent no one knows how long in learning to accept the aloneness and the darkness."

"I think you were right," said Cushing. "We could do nothing for it."

"Twice, in a small span of time," said Meg, "I have touched two intelligences: the brain case and the living rock, the boulder that we found. I told you that my powers are puny and the

87

touching of those two lives almost makes me wish I had no powers at all. It might be better not to know. The thing within the brain case fills me with sadness, and the rock, with fearfulness."

She shuddered. "That rock, laddie. It was old—so old, so hard, so cynical. Although cynical is not the word. Uncaring. Maybe that's the word. A thing filled with repulsive memories so old they are petrified. As if they came from someplace else. No memories such as could be produced upon the earth. From somewhere outside. From a place of everlasting night, where no sun has ever shone and there is no such thing as gladness."

They came upon only one person in their travel—a filthy old man who lived in a cave he had dug out of a hillside facing the river, the cave shored up with timbers, to provide a noisome den in which he could sleep or take shelter from the weather. Two lackadaisical hounds barked at the intruders, with a singular lack of enthusiasm, until the old man shushed them. The dogs settled down beside him, resuming their sleep, their hides twitching to dislodge the flies that settled on them. The man grinned, showing rotted teeth.

"Worthless," he said, nodding at the hounds. "Most worthless dawgs I ever had. Once they were good cooners, but now they've taken to treeing demons. Never knew there were so many demons in these parts. Of course, it's the demons' fault; they pester them dawgs. But it makes a man mad to spend the night out chasing coon, then find a demon up the tree. 'Tain't worth a man's time to kill one of them. There ain't nothing you can do with demons. They're so tough you can't cook them enough to get a tooth into them, and even if you could, the taste of them would turn your stomach over."

He continued, "You folks know, don't you, there's war parties on the prowl. Mostly they stay out on the prairie. No need of coming down here, because there's water to be found out there. Some big chief has got a burr underneath his tail and he's out to make some coup. Heading for the cities, more than likely. He's like to get his clock cleaned. Them city tribes are mean, I tell you. All sorts of dirty tricks. No thing like fighting fair. Any way to win. And I s'pose that's all right, although it leaves a bad taste in the mouth. Them war parties have been going through right sprightly for the last week or so. Thinning out a little now. In another week or two, you'll see them trailing back, rubbing out their tracks with their dragging rumps."

He spat into the dust and said, "What's that you got there with you? I been studying it and it makes no sort of sense. It looks plumb like one of those robots some people talk about from a long time back. My grandma, I remember, she had stories about robots. Stories about a lot of things, clacking all the time, always telling stories. But you know, even when I was a tad, I knew that they were only stories. There never was a lot of them things that she talked about. There never was no robots. I asked her where she heard them stories and she said her grandma had told them to her and that her grandma probably had heard them from her grandma. It do beat hell how old folks keep them stories going. You'd think that in time they'd just die out. But not, I guess, when there are so many grandmas clacking all the time."

He continued, "Would you folks be of a mind to break bread with me? It's almost that time now and I'd be proud to have you. I have a sack of fish and a haunch of coon that still is pretty fresh. . . ."

"No, thank you, sir," said Cushing. "We're in something of a hurry. We must be getting on."

Two days later, just before sunset, Cushing, traveling along the riverbank with Meg and Andy, glanced up at the bluff and saw Rollo tearing down it. He was coming fast, his metal body flashing in the light of the westering sun.

"There's something up," said Cushing. "There is some sort of trouble."

He looked around. In the last few days the river had narrowed and the bluffs on either side of it had grown less steep. A thin strip of trees still grew along the water's edge, but not the tall trees they had found farther down the stream. In the center of the river lay an island, a small one covered by a thick mat of willows.

"Meg," he said, "take Andy. Cross over to the island. Work as deep as you can into the willows and stay quiet. Keep Andy quiet. Don't let him make a sound. Get hold of his nostrils so he can't whicker."

"But, laddie boy—"

"Move, dammit. Don't stand there. Get over to that island. It's less than a hundred yards of water."

"But I can't swim," she wailed.

"It's shallow," he snapped. "You can walk it. It won't come up higher than your waist. Hang tight to Andy; if you get into trouble, he'll take you across."

"But—"

"Move!" he said, shoving at her.

Rollo was off the bluff, running like a whirlwind for the river. A flurry of dead leaves danced in his wake.

"A war party," he shouted. "Close behind me, coming fast."

"Did they see you?"

"I don't think so."

"Come on, then," said Cushing. "Hang tight to my belt. There's mud on the bottom. Try to keep your feet."

Meg and Andy, he saw, had almost reached the island. He

plunged into the water, felt the current take hold and tug at him.

"I'm hanging tight," said Rollo. "Even should I go down, I could crawl across the river, underwater. I would not drown. Breath I do not need."

Meg and Andy had reached the island and disappeared into the willows. Cushing, halfway across, glanced over his shoulder. There was no sign of anyone atop the bluff. A few more minutes, he thought. That is all I need.

They reached the island and plunged up the shelving bank, crawled into the willows.

"Now stay quiet," said Cushing. "Crawl over to Meg. Help her keep Andy quiet. There will be horses. He may try to talk to them."

Turning back, Cushing crept to the riverbank, staying low. Shielded by small sprays of the leafy willows, he looked across the river. There was no sign of anyone. A black bear had come down to the stream, just above the point where they had crossed, and stood there with a silly look upon his face, dipping first one paw, then the other, into the water, shaking each paw daintily as he took it out. The blufftop was empty. A few crows beat up toward it from the thin strip of woods that ran along the river, cawing plaintively.

Perhaps Rollow had been wrong, he told himself—not wrong about seeing the war band, but in calculating where they might be heading. Perhaps they had veered off before they reached the bluff. But even so, even if Rollo's calculation had been wrong, with a war party in the vicinity, it had not been a bad idea to go to cover. They had been lucky to have the island near, he thought. Unlike the valley farther down the river, there was not much cover here. Later, farther up the valley, there would be even less. They were getting deep into the prairie country and the valley would get even narrower and there'd be fewer trees. The time would come when they'd have to leave even the scanty cover that the valley offered and strike west across the plain.

He glanced up and down the river and saw that the bear had left. Some small animal, either mink or muskrat, probably a rat, had left the lower tip of the island and was angling down across the stream toward the bank, swimming strongly.

When he looked back at the blufftop, it was no longer empty. A small group of horsemen stood against the skyline, shouldered spears pointing at the sky. They sat motionless, apparently looking down into the valley. More came riding up and aligned themselves with those already there. Cushing held his breath. Was it possible that looking down at the river from their elevation, they could make out some sign of those who hid in the willows? Watching them closely, he could detect no sign that they could.

Finally, after long minutes, the horsemen began to come down the slope, the horses lurching over the edge of the bluff and coming down the slope in stiff-legged jumps. Most of the men, he saw, wore buckskins, darkened by work and weather. Some wore fur caps with the tails of wolf or fox or coon fluttering out behind. In some cases, similar animal tails were fastened to the shoulders of their buckskins. Others wore only leather trousers, the upper torso either bare or draped with furred robes or jackets. Most of them rode saddles, although there were a few bareback. Most carried spears; all had quivers, bristling with feathered arrows, at their backs.

They rode in deadly silence, with no banter back and forth. In an ugly mood, Cushing told himself, remembering what the old man had said about how they'd be coming back. And if that were the case, he knew, it had been doubly wise to get under cover. In such a mood, they'd be looking for someone upon whom they could vent their anger.

Behind the main band came a small string of packhorses, carrying leather sacks and bails, a few of the loads topped with carcasses of deer.

The party came down into the valley, swung slightly upstream into a grove of cottonwoods. There they stopped, dismounted, hobbled their horses and set about making camp. Now that they had stopped, there was some talk, the sound of it carrying down the river—but only talk, no shouting back and forth. Axes came into play, to cut wood for their fires, and the sound of chopping echoed between the encroaching bluffs.

Cushing backed away from the river's edge and made his way to where the others waited. Andy was lying down, nodding, his head half resting in Meg's lap.

"He's a lamb," said Meg. "I got him to lie down. It's safer that way, isn't it?"

Cushing nodded. "They're making camp just up the river. Forty or fifty of them. They'll be gone by morning light. We'll have to wait it out."

"You think they're dangerous, laddie?"

"I couldn't say," he told her. "They're quieter than they should be. No laughing, no joking, no shouting, no horseplay. They seem in an ugly mood. I think they took a licking at the City. Scratch one conqueror's itch for conquest. In that kind of situation, I'd just as soon not meet them."

"Come night," said Rollo, "I could cross the river and creep close up to their fires, listen to what they say. It would be nothing new for me. I've done it many times before, crawling upon campfires, lying there and listening, afraid to show myself but so starved for conversation, for the sound of voices, that I took the chance. Although there was really little chance, for I can be silent when I want to be and my eyes are as good at night as they are in daylight."

"You'll stay right here," said Cushing sharply. "There'll be no creeping up. By morning they'll be gone, and we can trail them for a while to see where they are going, then be on our way."

He slipped the knapsack off his shoulder and untied the thongs. He took out the chunk of jerky and, cutting off a piece of it, handed it to Meg.

"Tonight," he said, "this is your supper. Don't let me ever again hear you disparage it."

Night came down across the valley. In the darkness the river seemed to gurgle louder. Far off an owl began to chuckle. On the blufftop a coyote sang his yapping song. A fish splashed nearby and through the screening willows could be seen the flare of the campfire across the river. Cushing crept to the river's edge and stared across the water, at the camp. Dark figures moved about the fires and he caught the smell of frying meat. Off in the darkness horses moved restlessly, stamping and snorting. Cushing squatted in the willows for an hour or more, alert to any danger. When he was satisfied there seemed to be none, he made his way back to where Meg and Rollo sat with Andy.

Cushing made a motion toward the horse. "Is he all right?" he asked.

"I talked to him," said Meg. "I explained to him. He will give no trouble."

"No spells?" he asked, jokingly. "You put no spell upon him?"

"Perhaps a slight one, only. It will never harm him."

"We should get some sleep," he said. "How about it, Rollo? Can you watch the horse for us?"

Rollo reached out a hand and stroked Andy's neck. "He likes me," he said. "He is not frightened of me."

"Why should he be frightened of you?" asked Meg. "He knows you are his friend."

"Things at times are frightened of me," the robot said. "I

come in the general shape of men but I am not a man. Go on and sleep. I need no sleep. I will stay and watch. If need be, I will waken you."

"Be sure you do," said Cushing. "If there is anything at all. I think it is all right. Everything is quiet. They're settling down over there, across the river."

Wrapped in the blanket, he stared up through the willows. There was no wind and the leaves hung limply. Through them a few stars could be seen. The river murmured at him, talking its way down across the land. His mind cast back across the days and he tried to number them, but the numbers ran together and became a broad stream, like the river, slipping down the land. It had been good, he thought—the sun, the nights, the river and the land. There were no protective walls, no potato patches. Was this the way, he wondered, that a man was meant to live, in freedom and communion with the land, the water and the weather? Somewhere in the past, had man taken the wrong turning that brought him to walls, to wars and to potato patches? Somewhere down the river the owl heard earlier in the evening (could it be the same one?) chuckled, and far off a coyote sang in loneliness, and above the willows the stars seemed to leave their stations far in space and come to lean above him.

He was wakened by a hand that was gently shaking him.

"Cushing," someone was saying. "Cushing, come awake. The camp across the river. There is something going on."

He saw that it was Rollo, the starlight glinting on his metal. He half scrambled from the blanket. "What is it?" he asked.

"There's a lot of commotion. They are pulling out, I think. Dawn hours off and they are pulling out."

Cushing scrambled out of the blanket. "Okay, let us have a look."

Squatted at the water's edge, he stared across the river. The fires, burned low, were red eyes in the darkness. Hurrying figures moved darkly among them. The sound of stamping horses, the creak of saddle leather, but there was little talking.

"You're right," said Cushing. "Something spooked them."

"An expedition from the City? Following them?"

"Maybe," said Cushing. "I doubt it. If the city tribes beat them off, they'd be quite satisfied to leave them alone. But if these friends of ours across the river did take a beating, they'd be jumpy. They would run at shadows. They're in a hurry to get back to their old home grounds, wherever that may be."

Except for the muted noises of the camp and the murmur of the river, the land lay in silence. Both coyote and owl were quiet.

"We were lucky, sir," said Rollo.

"Yes, we were," said Cushing. "If they had spotted us, we might have been hard pressed to get away."

Horses were being led into the camp area and men were mounting. Someone cursed at his horse. Then they were moving out. Hoofs padded against the ground, saddle leather creaked, words went back and forth.

Cushing and Rollo squatted, listening as the hoofbeats receded and finally ceased.

"They'll get out of the valley as soon as they can," said Cushing. "Out on the prairie they can make better time."

"What do we do now?"

"We stay right here. A little later, just before dawn, I'll cross and scout. As soon as we know they're out on the prairie, we'll be on our way."

The stars were paling in the east when Cushing waded the stream. At the campsite the fires still smoked and cooling embers blinked among the ashes. Slipping through the trees, he found the trail, chewed by pounding hoofs, that the nomads had taken, angling up the bluff. He found the place where they had emerged upon the prairie and used the glasses to examine the wide sweep of rolling ground. A herd of wild cattle grazed in the middle distance. A bear was flipping over stones with an agile paw, to look for ants or grubs. A fox was slinking home after a night of hunting. Ducks gabbled in a tiny prairie pond. There were other animals, but no sign of humans. The nomads had been swallowed in the distance.

All the stars were gone and the east had brightened when he turned downhill for the camp. He snorted in disdain at the disorder of the place. No attempt had been made to police the grounds. Gnawed bones were scattered about the dead campfires. A forgotten double-bitted axe leaned against a tree. Someone had discarded a pair of worn-out moccasins. A buckskin sack lay beneath a bush.

He used his toe to push the sack from beneath the bush, knelt to unfasten the throngs, then seized it by the bottom and upended it.

Loot. Three knives, a small mirror in which the glass had become clouded, a ball of twine, a decanter of cut glass, a small metal fry-pan, an ancient pocket watch that probably had not run for years, a necklace of opaque red and purple beads, a thin, board-covered book, several folded squares of paper. A pitiful pile of loot, thought Cushing, bending over and sorting through it, looking at it. Not much to risk one's life and limb for. Although loot, he supposed, had been a small by-product, no more than souvenirs. Glory was what the owner of the bag had ridden for.

He picked up the book and leafed through the pages. A children's book from long ago, with many colored illustrations of imaginary places and imaginary people. A pretty book. Something to be shown and wondered over beside a winter campfire.

He dropped it on the pile of loot and picked up one of the

squares of folded paper. It was brittle from long folding—
perhaps for centuries—and required gingerly handling. Fold
by careful fold he spread it out, seeing as he did so that it was
more tightly folded and larger than he had thought. Finally the
last fold was free and he spread it out, still being careful of it. In
the growing light of dawn he bent close above it to make out
what it was and, for a moment, was not certain—only a flat and
time-yellowed surface with faint brown squiggle lines that ran
in insane curves and wiggles and with brown printing on it.
And then he saw—a topographical map, and, from the shape of
it, of the one-time state of Minnesota. He shifted it so he could
read the legends, and there they were—the Mississippi, the
Minnesota, the Mesabi and Vermilion ranges, Mille Lacs, the
North Shore. . . .

He dropped it and grabbed another, unfolded it more
rapidly and with less caution. Wisconsin. He dropped it in
disappointment and picked up the third. There were only two
others.

Let it be there, he prayed. Let it be there!

Before he had finished unfolding it, he knew he had what he
was looking for. Just across the great Missouri, Rollo had said,
and that had to be one of the Dakotas. Or did it have to be: It
could be Montana. Or Nebraska. Although, if he remembered
rightly from his reading, there were few buttes in Nebraska, or
at least few near the river.

He spread the South Dakota map flat on the ground and
smoothed it out, knelt to look at it. With a shaking finger he
traced out the snaky trail of the mighty river. And there it was,
west of the river and almost to the North Dakota line: THUNDER
BUTTE, with the legend faint in the weak morning light, with
the wide-spreading, close-together brown contour lines showing the shape and extent of it. Thunder Butte, at last!

He felt the surge of elation in him and fought to hold it

down. Rollo might be wrong. The old hunter who had told him might have been wrong—or worse, simply spinning out a story. Or this might be the wrong Thunder Butte; there might be many others.

But he could not force himself to believe these cautionary doubts. This was Thunder Butte, the right Thunder Butte. It had to be.

He rose, clutching the map in hand and faced toward the west. He was on his way. For the first time since he'd started, he knew where he was going.

14

A week later, they had traveled as far north as they could go. Cushing spread out the map to show them. "See, we've passed the lake. Big Stone Lake, it's called. There is another lake a few miles north of here, but the water flows north from it, into the Red. Thunder Butte lies straight west from here, perhaps a little north or a little south. Two hundred miles or so. Ten days, if we are lucky. Two weeks, more than likely." He said to Rollo, "You know this country?"

Rollo shook his head. "Not this country. Other country like it. It can be mean. Hard going."

"That's right," said Cushing. "Water may be hard to find. No streams that we can follow. A few flowing south and that is all. We'll have to carry water. I have this jacket and my pants. Good buckskin. There'll be some seepage through the leather, but not too much. They'll do for water bags."

"They'll do for bags," said Meg, "but poorly. You will die of sunburn."

"I worked all summer with the potatoes and no shirt. I am used to it."

"Your shirt only, then," she said. "Barbaric we may be, but I'll not have you prancing across two hundred miles without a stitch upon you."

"I could wear a blanket."

"A blanket would be poor clothing," Rollo said, "to go through a cactus bed. And there'll be cactus out there. There's no missing it. Soon I will kill a bear. I'm running low on grease. When I do, we can use the bearskin to make us a bag."

"Lower down the river," Cushing said, "there were a lot of bear. You could have killed any number of them."

"Black bear," said Rollo, with disdain. "When there are any others, I do not kill black bear. We'll be heading into grizzly country. Grizzly grease is better."

"You're raving mad," said Cushing. "Grizzly grease is no different from any other bear grease. One of these days, tangling with a grizzly, you'll get your head knocked off."

"Mad I may be," said Rollo, "but grizzly grease is better. And the killing of a black bear is as nothing to the killing of a grizzly."

"It seems to me," said Cushing, "that for a lowly robot you're a shade pugnacious."

"I have my pride," said Rollo.

They moved into the west, and every mile they moved, the land became bleaker. It was level land and seemed to run on forever, to a far horizon that was no more than a faint blue line against the blueness of the sky.

There were no signs of nomads; there had been none since that morning when the war party had moved so quickly out of camp. Now there were increasingly larger herds of wild cattle, with, here and there, small herds of buffalo. Occasionally, in the distance, they sighted small bands of wild horses. The deer had vanished; there were some antelope. Prairie chickens were plentiful and they feasted on them. They came on prairie-dog towns, acres of ground hummocked by the burrows of the little rodents. A close watch was kept for rattlesnakes, smaller than the timber rattlers they'd seen farther east. Andy developed a hatred for the buzzing reptiles, killing with slashing hoofs all that came within his reach. Andy, too, became their water hunter, setting out in a purposeful fashion and leading them to pitiful little streams or stagnant potholes.

"He can smell it out," said Meg, triumphantly. "I told you he would be an asset on our travels."

The Shivering Snake stayed with them now around the clock, circling Rollo and, at various times, Meg. She took kindly to it.

"It's so cute," she said.

And now, out in the loneliness, they were joined by something else—gray-purple shadows that slunk along behind them and on either side. At first they could not be sure if they were really shadows or only their imagination, born of the emptiness they traveled. But, finally, there could be no question of their actuality. They had no form or shape. Never for an instant could one gain a solid glimpse of them. It was as if a tiny cloud had passed across the sun to give rise to a fleeting shadow. But there were no clouds in the sky; the sun beat down mercilessly on them out of the brassy bowl that arced above their heads.

None of them spoke of it until one evening by a campfire located in a tiny glade, with a slowly trickling stream of reluctant water running along a pebbled creek bed, a small clump of plum bushes, heavy with ripened fruit, standing close beside the water.

"They're still with us," said Meg. "You can see them out there, just beyond the firelight."

"What are you talking about?" asked Cushing.

"The shadows, laddie boy. Don't pretend you haven't seen them. They've been stalking us for the last two days."

Meg appealed to Rollo. "You have seen them, too. More than likely, yóu know what they are. You've traveled up and down this land."

Rollo shrugged. "They're something no one can put a finger on. They follow people, that's all."

"But what are they?"

"Followers," said Rollo.

"It seems to me," said Cushing, "that on this trip we have had more than our share of strangenesses. A living rock, Shivering Snake and, now, the Followers."

"You could have passed that rock a dozen times," said Meg, "and not known what it was. It would have been just another rock to you. Andy sensed it first, then I. . . ."

"Yes, I know," said Cushing. "I could have missed the rock, but not the snake, nor the Followers."

"This is lonesome land," said Rollo. "It gives rise to many strangenesses."

"Everywhere in the West?" asked Cushing, "or this particular area?"

"Mostly here," said Rollo. "There are many stories told."

"Would it have something to do," asked Cushing, "with the Place of Going to the Stars?"

"I don't know," the robot said. "I know nothing about this Place of Going to the Stars. I only told you what I heard."

"It seems to me, Sir Robot," said Meg, "that you are full of evasiveness. Can you tell us further of the Followers?"

"They eat you," Rollo said.

"Eat us?"

"That is right. Not the flesh of you, for they have no need of flesh. The soul and mind of you."

"Well, that is fine," said Meg. "So we are to be eaten, the soul and mind of us, and yet you tell us nothing of it. Not until this minute."

"You'll not be harmed," said Rollo. "You'll still have mind and soul intact. They do not take them from you. They only savor of them."

"You have tried to sense them, Meg?" asked Cushing.

She nodded. "Confusing. Hard to come to grips with. As if there were more of them than there really are, although one never knows how many of them there really are, for you cannot count them. As if there were a crowd of them. As if there were a crowd of people, very many people."

"That is right," said Rollo. "Very many of them. All the people they have savored and made a part of them. For to start with, they are empty. They have nothing of their own. They're nobody and nothing. To become somebody, perhaps many somebodies—"

"Rollo," said Cushing, "do you know this for a fact, or are you only saying what you've heard from others?"

"Only what I have heard from others. As I told you, of evenings filled with loneliness, I'd creep up to a campfire and listen to all the talk that went back and forth."

"Yes, I know," said Cushing. "Tall tales, yarns. . . ."

Later that night, when Rollo had gone out for a scout-around, Meg said to Cushing, "Laddie buck, I am afraid."

"Don't let Rollo worry you," he said. "He's a sponge. He soaks up everything he hears. He makes no attempt to sort it out. He does not evaluate it. Truth, fiction—it is all the same to him."

"But there are so many strange things."

"And you, a witch. A frightened witch."

"I told you, remember, that my powers are feeble. A sensing power, a small reading of what goes through the mind. It was an act, I tell you. A way to be safe. To pretend to greater powers than I really had. A way to make the city tribes afraid to lay a hand upon me. A way to live, to be safe, to get gifts and food. A way of survival."

As they moved on, the land grew even more bleak. The horizons were far away. The sky stayed a steely blue. Strong winds blew from the north or west and they were dry winds, sucking up every drop of moisture, so that they moved through a blistering dryness. At times they ran short of water and then either Rollo would find it or Andy would sniff it from afar and they could drink again.

Increasingly, they came to feel they were trapped in the middle of an arid, empty loneliness from which there was no hope they ever would escape. There was an everlasting sameness: the cactus beds were the same; the sun-dried grass, the same; the little animal and bird life they encountered, unchanging.

"There are no bear," Rollo complained one night.

"Is that what you are doing all the time, running off?" asked Meg. "Looking for bear?"

"I need grease," he said. "My supply is running low. This is grizzly country."

"You'll find bear," said Cushing, "when we get across the Missouri."

"If we ever find the Missouri," said Meg.

And that was it, thought Cushing. In this place the feeling came upon you that everything you had ever known had somehow become displaced and moved; that nothing was where you had thought it was and that it probably never had been; that the one reality was this utter, everlasting emptiness that would go on forever and forever. They had walked out of old familiar Earth and, by some strange twist of fate or of circumstance, had entered this place that was not of Earth but was, perhaps, one of those far alien planets that at one time man may have visited.

Shivering Snake had formed itself into a sparkling halo that revolved sedately in the air just above Rollo's head, and at the edge of the farthest reach of firelight were flitting deeper shadows that were the Followers. Somewhere out there, he remembered, there was a place that he was seeking—not a place, perhaps, but a legend; and this place they traveled, as well, could be a legend. They—he and a witch and a robot, perhaps the last robot that was left; not the last left alive—for there were many of them that were still alive—but the last that was mobile, that could move about and work, the last that could see and hear and talk. And he and Meg, he thought— perhaps the only ones who knew the others were alive, prisoned in the soundless dark. A strange crew: a woods runner; a witch who might be a bogus witch, a woman who could be frightened, who had never voiced complaint at the hardship of the journey; an anachronism, a symbol of that other day when life might have been easier but had growing at its core a cancer that ate away at it until the easier life was no longer worth the living.

Now that the other, easier, cancer-ridden life was gone, he wondered, what about the present life? For almost fifteen centuries men had fumbled through a senseless and brutal barbarism and still wallowed in the barbarism. The worst of it, he told himself, was that there seemed to be no attempt to advance beyond the barbarism. As if man, failing in the course that he had taken, no longer had the heart nor the mind, perhaps not even the wish, to try to build another life. Or was it that the human race had had its chance and had muffed it, and there would not be another chance?

"Laddie, you are worried."

"No, not worried. Just thinking. Wondering. If we do find

the Place of Going to the Stars, what difference will it make?"

"We'll know that it is there. We'll know that, once, men traveled to the stars."

"But that's not enough," he said. "Just knowing's not enough."

The next morning his depression had vanished. There was, strangely enough, something exhilarating in the emptiness, a certain crispness and clearness, a spaciousness, that made one a lord of all that one surveyed. They were still alone, but it was not a fearsome aloneness; it was as if they moved across a country that had been tailor-made for them, a country from which all others had been barred, a far-reaching and far-seeing country. The Followers were still with them, but they no longer seemed to be a threat; rather, they were companions of the journey, part of the company.

Late in the day, they came upon two others, two human waifs as desolate as they in that vast stretch of emptiness. They saw them, when they topped a low swell, from half a mile away. The man was old; his hair and beard were gray. He was dressed in worn buckskins and stood as straight as a young oak tree, facing the west, the restless western wind tugging at his beard and hair. The woman, who appeared to be younger, was sitting to one side and behind him, her feet tucked beneath her, head and shoulders bent forward, covered by a ragged robe. They were situated beside a small patch of wild sunflowers.

When Cushing and the others came up to the two, they could see that the man was standing in two shallow holes that had been clawed out of the prairie sod, standing in them barefooted, with a pair of worn moccasins lying to one side. Neither he nor the woman seemed to notice their coming. The man stood straight and unmoving. His arms were folded across his chest; his chin tilted up and his eyes were shut. There was about him a sense of fine-edged alertness, as if he might be listening to something that no one else could hear. There was nothing to hear but the faint hollow booming of the wind as it raced across the land and an occasional rustle as it stirred the sunflower patch.

The woman, sitting cross-legged in the grass, did not stir. It was as if neither of them was aware they were no longer alone. The woman's head was bowed above her lap, in which her hands were loosely folded. Looking down at her, Cushing saw that she was young.

The three of them—Rollo, Meg, and Cushing—stood in a row, puzzled, slightly outraged, awaiting recognition. Andy switched flies and munched grass. The Followers circled warily.

It was ridiculous, Cushing told himself, that the three of them should be standing there like little naughty children who had intruded where they were not wanted and, for their trespass, were being studiously ignored. Yet there was an aura about the other two that prevented one from breaking in upon them.

While Cushing was debating whether he should be angry or abashed, the old man moved, slowly coming to life. First his arms unfolded and fell slowly, almost gracefully, to his sides. His head, which had been tilted back, inclined forward, into a more normal position. His feet lifted, one by one, out of the holes in which he had been standing. He turned his body, with a strange deliberation, so that he faced Cushing. His face was not the stern, harsh, patriarchal face that one might have assumed from watching him in his seeming trance but a kind, although sober, face—the face of a kindly man who had come to peace after years of hardship. Above his grizzled beard, which covered a good part of his face, a pair of ice-blue eyes, set off by masses of crow's feet, beamed out at the world.

"Welcome, strangers," he said, "to our few feet of ground. Would you have, I wonder, a cup of water for my granddaughter and myself?"

The woman still sat cross-legged on the grass, but now she raised her head and the robe that had covered it fell off, bunching at her back. Her face held a terrible sweetness and a horrible innocence and her eyes were blank. She was a prim-faced, pretty doll filled with emptiness.

"My granddaughter, if you failed to notice," said the old man, "is doubly blessed. She lives in another place. This world cannot touch her. Bespeak her gently, please, and have no concern about her. She is a gentle creature and there is nothing to be feared. She is happier than I am, happier than any one of us. Most of all, I ask you, do not pity her. It is the other way around. She, by all rights, could hold pity for the rest of us."

Meg stepped forward to offer him a cup of water, but he waved it away. "Elayne first," he said. "She is always first. And you may be wondering what I was doing, standing here in the holes I dug, and shut within myself. I was not as shut in as you might have thought. I was talking with the flowers. They are such pretty flowers and so sentient and well-mannered. . . . I almost said 'intelligent,' and that would not have been quite right, for their intelligence, if that is what you can call it, is not our intelligence, although, perhaps, in a way, better than our intelligence. A different kind of intelligence, although, come to think of it, 'intelligence' may not be the word at all."

"Is this a recent accomplishment," asked Cushing, with some disbelief, "or have you always talked with flowers?"

"More so now than was the case at one time," the old man told him. "I have always had the gift. Not only flowers, but trees and all other kinds of plants—grasses, mosses, vines, weeds, if any plant can rightly be called a weed. It's not so much that I talk with them, although at times I do. What I

109

mostly do is listen. There are occasions when I am sure they know that I am there. When this happens, I try to talk with them. Mostly I think they understand me, although I am not certain they are able to identify me, to know with any certainty what it is that is talking with them. It is possible their perceptions are not of an order that permits them to identify other forms of life. Largely, I am certain, they exist in a world of their own which is as blind to us as we are blind to them. Not blind in that we are unaware of them, for, to their sorrow, we are very much aware of them. What we are entirely blind to is the fact that they have a consciousness even as we have a consciousness."

"You'll pardon me," said Cushing, "if I seem unable immediately to grasp the full significance of what you're telling me. This is something that I have never thought of even in the wildest fantasies. Tell me—just now, were you listening only, or were you talking with them?"

"They were talking to me," said the old man. "They were telling me of a thing of wonder. To the west, they tell me, is a group of plants—I gather they are trees—that seem alien to this land, brought here many years ago. How brought, they do not know, or perhaps I only failed of understanding, but, in any case, great plants that stand as giants of understanding. . . . Ah, my dear, I thank you."

He took the cup from Meg and drank, not gulping it down but drinking it slowly, as if he were savoring every drop of it.

"To the west?" asked Cushing.

"Yes, to the west, they said."

"But . . . how would they know?"

"It seems they do. Perhaps seeds, flying in the wind, may carry word. Or wafting thistledown. Or passed along, one root to another. . . ."

"It's impossible," said Cushing. "It is all impossible."

"This metal creature, shaped in the form of man—what may it be?" the old man asked.

"I am a robot," Rollo said.

"Robots," said the old man. "Robots? Ah, yes, now I know. I've seen brain cases of robots, but not a living robot. So you are a robot?"

"My name is Rollo," the robot said. "I am the last one that there is. Although if I cannot find a bear . . ."

"My name is Ezra," said the old one. "I am an ancient wanderer. I wander up and down the land to converse with neighbors, wherever I may find them. This splendid patch of sunflowers, a vast stretch of tumbleweeds, a cluster of rosebushes, even the grass at times, although the grass has little to recommend itself. . . ."

"Grandfather," said Elayne, "put on your moccasins."

"So I shall," said Ezra. "I had quite forgotten them. And we must be on our way."

He scuffed his feet into the shapeless, battered moccasins.

"This is not the first time," he said, "that I have heard of this strange growing in the West. I heard of it first many years ago and wondered greatly at the news, although I did not act upon it. But now, with age fastening its bony grasp upon me, I do act upon the information. For if I fail to do so, perhaps no one else ever will. I have questioned widely and I know of no one else who can talk with plants."

"Now," said Meg, "you go to hunt these legendary plants."

He nodded his head. "I do not know if I shall find them, but we wander westward and I ask along the way. My people cried out against our going, for they thought it a foolish quest. Death along the trail, they said, was all that we would find. But once they saw that we were set upon the going, they urged us to accept an escort, a body of horsemen who, they said, would not interfere but would only accompany us at a distance to afford protection in case there should be danger. But we begged off from the escort. People of good heart can travel widely and no danger comes to them."

"Your people?" Meg asked.

"A tribe," said Ezra, "that lives in the prairies east of here, in a kinder land than this one. When we left, they offered horses and great stores of supplies, but we took none of them. We have a better chance of finding what we seek if we travel naked of all convenience. We carry nothing but a flint and steel with which to make a fire."

Cushing asked, "How do you manage to eat?"

"With great apology to our friends and neighbors, we subsist on roots and fruits we find along the way. I am sure our plant friends understand our need and harbor no resentment. I have tried to explain to them, and though they may not entirely understand, there has been no censure of us, no shrinking away in horror."

"You travel west, you say."

"We seek the strangeness of these plants somewhere in the West."

"We also travel west," said Cushing. "Both of us may be seeking different things, but what you tell us makes it seem we may find what each of us seeks in the same location. Would it be agreeable for you to travel with us? Or must you go alone?"

Ezra thought for a moment. Then he said, "It seems to me that it might be proper for all of us to go together. You seem plain and simple folk, with no evil in you. So we will gladly travel with you upon one condition."

"And that condition?"

"That occasionally, on the way, I may stop for a while to talk with my friends and neighbors."

15

West of the river, the land heaved up in tortuous, billowing surges to reach the dry emptiness of the high plains.

From where he stood, Cushing looked down to the yellow streak of river, a smooth and silky ribbon of water that held in it something of the appearance of a snake, or of a mountain lion. So different here from what it had been during the days they had camped upon its bank, resting for this, the final lap of their journey—if, indeed, it should be the final lap. Viewed close at hand, the river was a sand-sucking, roiling, pugnacious terror, a raucous, roistering flood of water that chewed its way down across the land. Strange, he thought, how rivers could have such distinctive characteristics—the powerful, solemn thrust of the upper Mississippi; the chuckling, chattering comradeship of the Minnesota; and this, the rowdy bellicosity of the Missouri.

Rollo had lit the evening fire in a swale that ran down a slope, selecting a place where they would have some protection from

the wind that came howling and whooping from the great
expanse of prairie that stretched for miles into the west. Looking west, away from the river, one could see the continuing
uplift, the rising land that swooped and climbed in undulating
folds, to finally terminate in the darkness of a jagged line
imprinted against the still-sunlit western sky. Another day,
Cushing figured, until they reached the plains country. So
long, he thought, it had taken so long—the entire trip much
longer than it should have been. Had he traveled alone, he'd
be there by now, although, come to think of it, traveling alone,
he might have no idea of the location of the place he sought. He
pondered for a moment that strange combination of circumstances which had led to his finding of Rollo, in whose mind
had stuck the name of Thunder Butte; and then the finding of
the geological-survey maps, which had shown where Thunder
Butte—or, at least, where one of many possible Thunder
Buttes—might be found. Traveling alone, he realized, he
might have found neither Rollo nor the maps.

The progress of the expedition had been slower since the
addition of the old man and the girl, with Ezra digging holes in
which to stand, to talk with or listen to (or whatever it was he
did) a patch of cactus or a clump of tumbleweed, or flopping
down into a sitting posture, to commune with an isolated bed of
violets. Standing by, gritting his teeth, more times than he
liked to think of, Cushing had suppressed an impulse to kick
the old fool into motion or simply to walk away and leave him.
Despite all this, however, he had to admit that he liked Ezra
well enough. Despite his obstinate eccentricities, he was a
wise, and possibly clever, old man who generally had his wits
about him except for his overriding obsession. He sat at nights
beside the campfire and talked of olden times when he had
been a great hunter and, at times, a warrior, sitting in council
with other, older tribal members when a council should be

needed, with the realization creeping on him only gradually that he had an uncommon way with plant life. Once this had become apparent to other members of the tribe, his status gradually changed, until finally he became, in the eyes of the tribe, a man wise and gifted beyond the ordinary run of men. Apparently, although he talked little of it, the idea of going forth to wander and commune with plants and flowers also had come upon him slowly, a conviction growing with the years until he reached a point where he could see quite clearly he was ordained for a mission and must set forth upon it, not with the pomp and grandeur that his fellow tribesmen gladly would have furnished, but humbly and alone except for that strange granddaughter.

"She is a part of me," he'd say. "I cannot tell you how, but unspoken between us is an understanding that cannot be described."

And while he talked, of her or of other things, she sat at the campfire with the rest of them, relaxed, at peace, her hands folded in her lap, at times her head bent almost as if in prayer, at other times lifted and held high, giving the impression that she was staring, not out into the darkness only but into another world, another place or time. On the march, she moved lightly of foot—there were times when she seemed to float rather than to walk—serene and graceful, and more than graceful, a seeming to be full of grace, a creature set apart, a wild sprite that was human in a tantalizing way, a strange, concentrated essence of humanity that stood and moved apart from the rest of them, not because she wished to do so but because she had to do so. She seldom spoke. When she did speak, it was usually to her grandfather. It was not that she ignored the rest of them but that she seldom felt the need to speak to them. When she spoke, her words were clear and gentle, perfectly and correctly spoken, not the jargon or the mumbling of the mentally deficient, which she at times appeared to be, leaving all of them wondering if she were or not, and, if so, what kind of direction the deficiency might take.

Meg was with her often, or she with Meg. Watching the two of them together, walking together or sitting together, Cushing often tried to decide which of them it was who was with the other. He could not decide; it was as if some natural magnetic quality pulled the two of them together, as if they shared some common factor that made them move to each other. Not that they ever really met; distance, of a sort, always separated them. Meg might speak occasionally to Elayne, but not often, respecting the silence that separated them—or the silence that, at times, could make them one. Elayne, for her part, spoke no oftener to Meg than she did to any of the others.

"The wrongness of her, if there is a wrongness," Meg once said to Cushing, "is the kind of wrongness that more of us should have."

"She lives within herself," said Cushing.

"No," said Meg. "She lives outside herself. Far outside herself."

When they reached the river, they set up camp in a grove of cottonwoods growing on a bank that rose a hundred feet or so above the stream, a pleasant place after the long trek across the barren prairie. Here, for a week, they rested. There were deer in the breaks of the bluffs that rimmed the river's eastern edge. The lowlands swarmed with prairie chicken and with ducks that paddled in the little ponds. There were catfish in the river. They lived well now, after scanty fare.

Ezra established rapport with a massive cottonwood that bore the scars of many seasons, standing for hours on end, facing the tree and embracing it, communing with it while its wind-stirred leaves seemed to murmur to him. So long as he was there, Elayne was there as well, sitting a little distance off, cross-legged on the ground, the moth-eaten elkskin pulled up about her head, her hands folded in her lap. At times, Shivering Snake deserted Rollo and stayed with her, spinning and dancing all about her. She paid it no more attention than the rest of them. At other times, the Followers, purple blobs of shadow, sat in a circle about her, like so many wolves waiting for a feast, and she paid them no more attention than she paid Shivering Snake. Watching her, Cushing had the startling thought that she paid them no attention because she had recognized them for what they were and dismissed them from her thoughts.

Rollo hunted grizzly, and for a couple of days Cushing went out to help him hunt. But there were no grizzlies; there were no bear of any kind.

"The oil is almost gone," wailed Rollo. "I'm already getting squeaky. Conserving it, I use less than I should."

"The deer I killed was fat," said Cushing.

"Tallow!" Rollo cried. "Tallow I won't use."

"When the oil is gone, you'll damn well use whatever comes to hand. You should have killed a bear back on the Minnesota. There were a lot of them."

"I waited for the grizzly. And now there are no grizzlies."

"That's all damn foolishness," said Cushing. "Grizzly oil is no different from the oil from any other bear. You're not clear out, are you?"

"Not entirely. But nothing in reserve."

"We'll find grizzly west of the river," said Cushing.

Andy had eaten the scant bitter prairie grass in the East with reluctance, consuming only enough of it to keep life within his body. Now he stood knee-deep in the lush grass of the valley. With grunts of satisfaction, his belly full to bulging, he luxuriated by rolling on the sandy beach that ran up from the river's edge, while killdeer and sandpiper, outraged by his invasion of their domain, went scurrying and complaining up and down the sands.

Later Andy helped Rollo and Cushing haul in driftwood deposited by earlier floods on the banks along the river. Out of the driftwood Cushing and Rollo constructed a raft, chopping the wood into proper lengths and lashing the pieces together as securely as possible with strips of green leather cut from the hides of deer. When they crossed the river, Rollo and Meg rode the raft—Meg because she couldn't swim, Rollo because he was afraid of getting wet since his oil supply was low. The others clung to the raft. It helped them with their swimming and they tried as best they could to drive it across the stream and keep it from floating too far down the river. Andy, hesitant to enter the swift-flowing water, finally plunged in and swam so lustily that he outdistanced them and was waiting for them on the other side, nickering companionably at them when they arrived.

Since that mid-morning hour, they had climbed steadily. Ezra, for once, had not insisted on stopping to talk with plants. Behind them the river had receded slowly; ahead of them the great purple upthrust never seemed closer.

Cushing walked down the short slope of ground to reach the evening fire. Tomorrow, he thought, tomorrow we may reach the top.

Five days later, from far off, they sighted Thunder Butte. It was no more than a smudge on the northern horizon, but the smudge, they knew, could be nothing other than the butte; there was nothing else in this flat emptiness that could rise up to make a ripple on the smooth circle of horizon.

Cushing said to Meg, "We've made it. We'll be there in a few more days. I wonder what we'll find."

"It doesn't matter, laddie boy," she told him. "It's been a lovely trip."

16

Three days later, with Thunder Butte looming large against
the northern sky, they found the wardens waiting for them.
The five wardens sat their horses at the top of a slight billowing
rise, and when Cushing and the others approached them, one
of them rode forward, his left hand lifted, open-palmed, in a
sign of peace.

"We are the wardens," he said. "We keep the faith. We
mount guard against wanderers and troublemakers."

He didn't look much like a warden, although Cushing was
not quite sure how a warden should look. The warden looked
very much like a nomad who had fallen on hard times. He
carried no spear, but there was a quiver resting on his back,
with a short bow tucked in among the arrows. He wore woolen
trousers, out at the knees and ragged at the cuffs. He had no
jacket, but a leather vest that had known better days. His horse
was a walleyed mustang that at one time might have had the

devil in him, but was now so broken down that he was beyond all menace.

The other four, sitting their nags a few paces off, looked in no better shape.

"We are neither wanderers nor troublemakers," Cushing said, "so you have no business with us. We know where we are going and we want no trouble."

"Then you had best veer off," the warden said. "If you go closer to the butte, you will be causing trouble."

"This is Thunder Butte?" asked Cushing.

"That is what it is," the warden said. "You should have known that if you had been watching it this morning. There was a great black cloud passing over it, with lightning licking at its top, and the thunder rolling."

"We saw it," Cushing said. "We wondered if that is how it got its name."

"Day after day," the warden said, "there is this great black cloud. . . ."

"What we saw this morning," said Cushing, "was no more than a thunderstorm that missed us, passing to the north."

"You mistake me, friend," the warden said. "It's best we palaver." He made a sign to the other four and slid down off his horse. He ambled forward and squatted. "You might as well hunker down," he said, "and let us have a talk."

The other four came up and hunkered down beside him. The first man's horse wandered back to join its fellows.

"Well, all right," said Cushing, "we'll sit a while with you, if that is what you want. But we can't stay long. We have miles to cover."

"This one?" asked the warden, making a thumb at Rollo. "I never saw one like him before."

"He's all right," said Cushing. "You have no need to worry."

Looking at the five of them more closely, he saw that except for one roly-poly man, the rest of them were as gaunt and grim as scarecrows, as if they had been starved almost to emaciation. Their faces were little more than skulls with brown, parchmentlike skin stretched tightly over bone. Their arms and legs were pipestems.

From the slight rise of ground, Thunder Butte could be plainly seen, a dominant feature that rose above all the terrible flatness. Around its base ran a darker ring that must be the trees that Rollo had said formed a protective circle about it—and more than likely Ezra's trees as well, although perhaps not exactly the kind of trees that Ezra claimed the sunflowers and the other plants had told him.

"This morning," Cushing said to the squatting wardens, "through the glasses, I caught a glimpse of whiteness at the very top of Thunder Butte. They had the look of buildings, but I could not be certain. Do you know if there are buildings up there?"

"There are magic habitations," said the spokesman of the group. "There sleep the creatures that will follow men."

"How do you mean, 'will follow men'?"

"When men are gone, they will come forth and take the place of men. Or, if they wake first, even before the last of men are gone, they will come forth and displace men. They will sweep men off the earth and take their place."

"You say that you are wardens," Meg said to them. "Do you mean you guard these creatures, that you keep them free of interference?"

"Should anyone approach too closely," said the warden, "they might awake. And we do not want them to awake. We want them to sleep on. For, once they wake and emerge, men's days on Earth are numbered."

"And you are on patrol to warn anyone who comes too close?"

"For centuries on centuries," said the warden, "we have kept patrol. This is but one patrol; there are many others. It takes a great many of us to warn wanderers away. That is why we stopped you. You had the appearance of heading for the butte."

"That is right," said Cushing. "We are heading for the butte."

"There is no use of going there," the warden said. "You can never reach the butte. The Trees won't let you through. And even if the Trees don't stop you, there are other things that will. There are rocks to break your bones. . . ."

"Rocks!" cried Meg.

"Yes, rocks. Living rocks that keep watch with the Trees."

"There, you see!" Meg said to Cushing. "Now we know where that boulder came from."

"But that was five hundred miles away," said Cushing. "What would a rock be doing there?"

"Five hundred miles is a long way," said the warden, "but the rocks do travel. You say you found a living rock? How could you know it was a living rock? They aren't any different; they look like any other rock."

"I could tell," said Meg.

"The Trees shall let us through," said Ezra. "I shall talk with them."

"Hush, Grandfather," said Elayne. "These gentlemen have a reason for not wanting us to go there. We should give them hearing."

"I have already told you," said the warden, "we fear the Sleepers will awake. For centuries we have watched—we and those other generations that have gone before us. The trust is handed on, from a father to his son. There are old stories, told centuries ago, about the Sleepers and what will happen when they finish out their sleep. We keep the ancient faith. . . ."

The words rolled on—the solemn, dedicated words of a man sunk deep in faith. The words, thought Cushing, paying slight attention to them, of a sect that had twisted an ancient fable into a body of belief and a dedication that made them owe their lives to the keeping of that mistaken

The sun was sinking in the west and its slanting light threw the landscape into a place of tangled shadows. Beyond the rise on which they squatted, a deep gully slashed across the land, and along the edges of it grew thick tangles of plum trees. In the far distance a small grove of trees clustered, perhaps around a prairie pond. But except for the gully and its bushes and the stand of distant trees, the land was a gentle ocean of dried and withered grass that ran in undulating waves toward the steep immensity of Thunder Butte.

Cushing rose from where he had been squatting and moved over to one side of the two small groups facing one another. Rollo, who had not squatted with the others but had remained standing a few paces to the rear, moved over to join him.

"Now what?" the robot asked.

"I'm not sure," said Cushing. "I don't want to fight them. From the way they act, they don't want any fighting, either. We could just settle down, I suppose, and try to wear them out with waiting, but I don't think that would work. And there's no arguing with them. They are calm and conceited fanatics who believe in what they're doing."

"They aren't all that tough," said Rollo. "With a show of force . . ."

Cushing shook his head. "Someone would get hurt."

Elayne rose to her feet. Her voice came to them, calm, unhurried, so precise it hurt. "You are wrong," she said to the wardens. "The things you have been telling us have no truth in them. There are no Sleepers and no danger. We are going on."

With that, she walked toward them, slowly, deliberately, as

if there were no one there to stop her. Meg rose swiftly, clutching at her arm, but Elayne shook off the hand. Ezra came quickly to his feet and hurried to catch up with Elayne. Andy flicked his tail and followed close behind.

The wardens sprang up quickly and began to back away, their eyes fastened on the terrible gentleness of Elayne's face.

From off to one side came a coughing roar and Cushing spun around to face in its direction. A huge animal, gray and brown, humped of shoulder, great mouth open in its roar, had burst from a clump of plum bushes that grew beside the gully and was charging the wardens' huddled horses. The horses, for an instant, stood frozen in their fear, then suddenly reacted, plunging in great arcing leaps to escape the charging bear.

Rollo catapulted into action, at full speed with his second stride; his spear, held two-handed, extended straight before him.

"A grizzly!" he shouted. "After all this time, a grizzly!"

"Come back, you fool," yelled Cushing, reaching for an arrow and nocking it to the bowstring.

The horses were running wildly. Straight behind them came the bear, screaming in his rage, rapidly closing on the frightened animals. Running directly at the bear was Rollo, with leveled spear thrusting out toward it.

Cushing raised the bow and drew back the arrow, almost to his cheek. He let it go and the arrow was a whicker in the golden sunshine of late afternoon. It struck the bear in the neck and the bear whirled, roaring horribly. Cushing reached for another arrow. As he raised the bow again, he saw the bear, rearing on its hind legs, its face a foaming frenzy, its forelegs lifted to strike down, with Rollo almost underneath them, the spear thrusting up to strike. Out of the tail of his eye, Cushing saw Andy, head stretched forward, ears laid back, tail streaming out behind him, charging down at full gallop upon the embattled bear.

Cushing let the arrow go and heard the thud, saw its feathered end protruding from the bear's chest, just below the neck. Then the bear was coming down, its forearms reaching out to grasp Rollo in their clutches, but with Rollo's spear now buried deeply in its chest. Andy spun on his front legs, his hind legs lashing out. They caught the bear's belly with a sickening, squashy sound.

The bear was down and Rollo was scrambling out from underneath it, the bright metal of his body smeared with blood. Andy kicked the bear again, then trotted off, prancing, his neck bowed in pride. Rollo danced a wild war jig around the fallen bear, whooping as he danced.

"Grease!" he was yelling. "Grease, grease, grease!"

The bear kicked and thrashed in reflex action. The wardens' horses were rapidly diminishing dots on the prairie to the south. The wardens, running desperately behind them, were slightly larger dots.

"Laddie boy," Meg said, watching them, "I would say this broke up the parley."

"Now," said Elayne, "we'll go on to the butte."

"No," said Cushing. "First we render out some oil for Rollo."

17

As the wardens had said, the living rocks were waiting for them, just outside the Trees. There were dozens of them, with others coming up from either side, rolling sedately, with a flowing, effortless, apparently controlled motion, moving for a time, then stopping, then rolling once again. They were dark of color, some of them entirely black, and they measured—or at least the most of them measured—up to three feet in diameter. They did not form a line in front of the travelers, to block their way, but moved out, to range themselves around them, closing to the back of them and to each side, as if they were intent upon herding them toward the Trees.

Meg moved close to Cushing. He put his hand upon her arm and found that she was shivering. "Laddie buck," she said, "I feel the coldness once again, the great uncaring. Like the time we found the rock on the first night out."

"It'll be all right," he said, "if we can make our way through the Trees. The rocks seem to want us to move in toward the Trees."

"But the wardens said the Trees would not let us through."

"The wardens," he said, "are acting out an old tradition that may not have any meaning now or may never have had a meaning, something that they clung to through the centuries because it was the one reality they had, the one thing in which they could believe. It gave them a sense of continuity, a belonging to the ancient past. It was something that set them apart as special people and made them important."

"And yet," said Meg, "when the bear stampeded the horses, they left us and went streaking after them, and they've not been back."

"I think it was Elayne," said Cushing. "Did you see their faces when they looked at her? They were terrified. The bear, running off the horses, took them off a psychological hook and gave them an excuse to get out of there."

"Maybe, too," said Meg, "it was being without horses. To the people of the plains, a horse is an important thing. They're crippled without horses. Horses are a part of them. So important that they had to run after them, no matter what."

The Trees loomed before them, a solid wall of greenery, with the greenery extending down to the very ground. They had the look of a gigantic hedge. There was an ordinary look about them, like any other tree, but Cushing found himself unable to identify them. They were hardwoods, but they were neither oak nor maple, elm nor hickory. They were not exactly like any other tree. Their leaves, stirring in the breeze, danced and talked the language of all trees, although, listening to them, Cushing gained the impression they were saying something, that if his ears had been sharp enough and attuned to the talk that they were making, he could understand the words.

Shivering Snake, positioned in a halo just above Rollo's

head, was spinning so fast that in one's imagination one could hear it whistle with its speed. The Followers had come in closer, smudged shadows that dogged their heels, as if they might be staying close to seek protection.

Ezra had halted not more than ten feet from the green hedge of the Trees and had gone into his formal stance, standing rigidly, with his arms folded across his chest, his head thrown back, his eyes closed. Slightly behind him and to one side, Elayne had flopped down to the ground, feet tucked beneath her, hands folded in her lap, and bowed, with the ragged elkskin pulled up to cover her.

Now there was a new sound, a faint clicking that seemed to come from back of them, and when Cushing turned to see what it might be, he saw it was the rocks. They had joined in a semicircular formation, extending from the forefront of the Trees on one hand, around an arc to the forefront of the Trees on the other hand, spaced equidistantly from one another, no more than a foot or so apart, forming an almost solid line of rocks, hemming in the travelers, holding them in place. The clicking, he saw, resulted when the rocks, each one standing in its place, but each one rocking slightly, first to one side, then the other, struck against the neighbors next in line.

"It's horrible," said Meg. "That coldness—it is freezing me."

The tableau held. Ezra stood rigid; Elayne sat unmoving; Andy switched a nervous tail. The Followers came in closer, now actually among them, blobs of shadows that seemed to merge with the others huddled there. Shivering Snake outdid itself in its frantic spinning.

Rollo said, softly, "We are not alone. Look back of us."

Cushing and Meg twisted around to look. Half a mile away, five horsemen sat their mounts, graven against the skyline.

"The wardens," said Meg. "What are they doing here?"

As she spoke, the wardens raised a wail, a lonesome, forsaken lament, a thin keening in which was written an ultimate despair.

"My God, laddie boy," said Meg, "will there never be an end to it?"

And, saying that, she deliberately strode forward until she stood beside Ezra, raising her arms in a supplicating pose.

"In the name of all that's merciful," she cried, "let us in! Please, do let us in!"

The Trees seemed to come alive. They stirred, their branches rustling and moving to one side to form a doorway so the travelers could come in.

They walked into a place where lay a templed hush, a place from which the rest of the world seemed forever sealed. Here was no low-hanging greenery but a dark and empty vastness that rose up above them, a vastness supported by enormous tree boles that went up and up into the dimness, like clean churchly pillars that soared into the upper reaches of a sainted edifice. Beneath their feet was the carpetlike duff of a forest floor—the cast-off debris that had fallen through the centuries and lain undisturbed. Behind them the opening closed, the outer greenery falling into place.

They halted, standing in the silence that they discovered was really not a silence. From far above came the soughing of trees put in motion by the wind, but, strangely, the soughing did no more than emphasize the basic hush that held here in the dimness.

Well, we made it, Cushing thought to say, but the deep hush and the dimness strangled him and no words came out. Here was not a place where one engaged in idle conversation. Here was something that he had not bargained for, that he had never dreamed. He'd set out on a forthright quest for a Place of Going to the Stars, and even in those times when he could bring himself to think that he had a chance of finding it, he had thought of it as being a quite ordinary installation from which men had launched their great ships into space. But the Trees and the living rocks, even the wardens, had about them a touch of fantasy that did not square with the place he had sought to find. And if this butte was, in all reality, the Place of Going to the Stars, what the hell had happened?

Ezra was on his knees and his lips were moving, but the words he spoke, if he was speaking words, were mumbled.

"Ezra," Cushing asked sharply, "what is going on?"

Elayne was not sitting with her grandfather, as had been her habit, but was standing over him. Now she turned to Cushing. "Leave him alone," she said coldly. "Leave him alone, you fool."

Meg plucked at Cushing's sleeve. "The Holy of Holies?" she asked.

"What in the name of God are you talking about?"

"This place. It is the Holy of Holies. Can't you feel it?"

He shook his head. To him there seemed nothing holy about it. Frightening, yes. Forsaken, yes. A place to get away from as soon as one was able. A place of quiet that suddenly seemed to hold a strange unquietness. But nothing that was holy.

You are right, the Trees said to him. *There is nothing holy here. This is the place of truth. Here we find the truth; here we extract the truth. This is the place of questioning, of examination. This is where we look into the soul.*

For an instant he seemed to see (in his imagination?) a grim and terrible figure dressed in black, with a black cowl that came down about a bony face that was merciless. The figure and the face struck terror into him. His legs were watery and bending; his body drooped and his brain became a blob of shaking jelly. His life, all his life, everything that he had ever been or seen or done, spilled out of him, and although it was out of him, he could feel sticky fingers with unclean fingernails plucking at it busily, sorting it out, probing it, examining it, judging it and then balling it all together in a scrawny, bony fist and stuffing it back into him again.

He stumbled forward on jerky legs that still seemed watery, and only by the greatest effort kept himself from falling. Meg was beside him, holding him and helping him, and in that moment his heart went out to her—this marvelous old hag who had trod uncomplainingly all the weary miles that had led them to this place.

"Straight ahead, laddie boy," she said. "The way is open now. Just a little farther."

Through bleary eyes he saw ahead of him an opening, a tunnel with light at its other end, not just a little way, as she had said, but some distance off. He staggered on, with Meg close beside him, and although he did not look back to see—fearful that, looking back, he would lose the way—he knew that the others were coming on behind him.

Time stretched out, or seemed to stretch out, and then the tunnel's mouth was just ahead of him. With a final effort he lurched through it and saw ahead of him a rising slope of ground that went up and never seemed to stop, ground covered with the beautiful tawniness of sun-dried grass, broken by rocky ledges thrusting from the slope, dotted by clumps of bushes and here and there a tree.

Behind him Rollo said, "We made it, boss. We are finally here. We are on Thunder Butte."

18

A short distance up the slope, they found a pool of water in a rock basin fed by a stream that barely trickled down a deep gully, with misshapen, wind-tortured cedars forming a half-hearted windbreak to the west. Here they built a meager fire of dead branches broken off the cedar trees, and broiled steaks cut off a haunch of venison that was on the point of becoming high.

They were up the slope far enough that they could see over the ring of the Trees to the plains beyond. There, just over the tip of the Trees, could be seen the toylike figures of the wardens. Their horses were bunched off to one side and the five wardens stood in line, facing toward the butte. At times they would fling their arms up in unison, and at other times, when the wind died down momentarily, those around the fire could hear their shrill keening.

Meg studied them through the glasses. "It's some sort of

lament," she said. "Rigid posturing, then a little dance step or two, then they throw up their arms and howl."

Ezra nodded gravely. "They are devoted but misguided men," he said.

Cushing growled at him. "How the hell do you know? You are right, of course, but tell me how you know. I don't mind telling you that I have a belly full of your posturing, which is as bad as anything the wardens may be doing."

"You do me wrong," said Ezra. "I was the one who got us through the Trees. I spoke to them and they opened a way for us; then I spoke to them again and they let us out."

"That's your version," said Cushing. "Mine is that Meg got us in, then got us out again. All you did was mumble."

"Laddie boy," said Meg, "let's not quarrel among ourselves. It doesn't really matter who got us through the Trees. The important thing is they did let us through."

Elayne looked at Cushing and for once her eyes had no blankness in them. They were cold with hatred. "You have never liked us," she said. "You have patronized us, made fun of us. I'm sorry that we joined you."

"Now, now, my pet," said Ezra, "we all are under tension, but the tension now is gone, or should be. I'll admit that I may have been over-clowning to a small degree, although I swear to you that my belief in my own ability has not faded; that I believe, as always, that I can talk with plants. I did talk with the Trees; I swear I talked with them and they talked to me. In a different way from the way any plant has ever talked with me before. A sharper conversation, not all of which I understood, a great part of which I did not understand. They talked of concepts that I have never heard before, and though I knew they were new and important, I could grasp but the very edges of them. They looked deep inside of me and let me look, for a little distance, into them. It was as if they were examining

133

me—not my body but my soul—and offered me a chance to do the same with them. But I did not know how to go about it; even with them trying to show me, I did not know the way to go about it."

"Space is an illusion," said Elayne, speaking in a precise textbook voice, as if she were speaking not to them, nor indeed to anyone, but was merely reciting something that she knew or had newly learned, speaking as if it were a litany. "Space is an illusion, and time as well. There is no such factor as either time or space. We have been blinded by our own cleverness, blinded by false perceptions of those qualities that we term eternity and infinity. There is another factor that explains it all, and once this universal factor is recognized, everything grows simple. There is no longer any mystery, no longer any wonder, no longer any doubt; for the simplicity of it all lies before us—the simplicity . . . the simplicity . . . the simplicity . . ."

Her voice ran down on the single word and she lapsed into silence. She sat staring out beyond the campfire circle, her hands folded in her lap, her face again assuming the look of horrifying emptiness and terrible innocence.

The rest of them sat silent, stricken, and from somewhere a chill came off the slope of ground above them and held them motionless with an uncomprehending dread.

Cushing shook himself, asked in a strained voice, "What was that all about?"

Ezra made a motion of resignation. "I don't know. She has never done a thing like that before."

"Poor child," said Meg.

Ezra spoke angrily. "I've told you before, I tell you now: never pity her; rather, it is she who should pity us."

Meg said, "No pity was intended."

"There are more wardens out there," said Rollo. "A new band of them just showed up. Six or seven, this time. And from far to the east there seems to be others coming in. A great dust cloud, but I can see no more."

"It was a shame about the wardens," said Meg. "We messed them up after all their years of watching. All those generations and no one had ever got through."

"Perhaps there has never been anyone before who wanted to," said Rollo.

"That may be true," said Meg. "No one who wanted to get through as badly as we wanted to. No one with a purpose."

"If it hadn't been for the bear," said Rollo, "we might not have made it, either. The bear provided a distraction. And they lost their horses. They were naked and defenseless without the horses."

"The bear shook them up," said Ezra. "No man in his right mind goes against a bear with nothing but a spear."

"I'm not a man," said Rollo, reasonably, "and I was not alone. Cushing put some arrows in the beast and even Andy came in on the kill."

"My arrows did nothing," said Cushing. "They only irritated him."

He rose from where he was sitting and went up the slope, climbing until the campfire was no more than a small red eye glowing in the dusk. He found a small rock-ledge that cropped out from the slope, and sat upon it. The dusk was deepening into night. The Trees were a hump of blackness and out beyond them what must have been the campfires of the wardens flickered on and off, sometimes visible, sometimes not.

Sitting on the ledge, Cushing felt an uneasy peace. After miles of river valley and of high dry plains, they had finally reached the place where they were going. The goal had been reached and the daily expectation of reaching it had vanished and there seemed to be little to fill the void that was left by the lapsing of the expectations. He wondered about that, a bit confused. When one reached a goal, there should be, if nothing else, at least self-congratulation.

Below him, something grated on a stone, and when he looked in that direction, he made out the dull gleam of something moving. Watching, he saw that it was Rollo.

The robot came up the last few paces and without a word sat down on the ledge beside Cushing. They sat for a moment in silence; then Cushing said, "Back there, a while ago, you called me boss. You should not have done that. I'm not any boss."

"It just slipped out," said Rollo. "You ran a good safari—is that the right word? I heard someone use it once. And you got us here."

"I've been sitting here and thinking about getting here," said Cushing. "Worrying a little about it."

"You shouldn't be doing any worrying," said Rollo. "This is the Place of Going to the Stars."

"That's what I'm worrying about. I'm not so sure it is. It's something, but I'm fairly sure it's not the Place of Stars. Look, to go to the stars, to send ships into space, you need launching pads. This is not the kind of place to build launching pads. Up on top of the butte, perhaps, if there is any level ground up there, you might build launching pads. But why on top of a butte? The height of the land would be no advantage. The job of getting materials up to the launching site . . . It would be ridiculous to put pads up there when out on the plains you have thousands of acres of level ground."

"Well, I don't know," said Rollo. "I don't know about such things."

"I do," said Cushing. "Back at the university, I read about the moon shots and the Mars shots and all the other shots. There were a number of articles and books that told how it was done, and it was not done from atop a hill."

"The Trees," said Rollo. "Someone put the Trees around the butte—all around the butte—to protect whatever may be here. Maybe before the Time of Trouble, the people got up in arms against going to the stars."

"That might have been so," said Cushing. "Protection might have been needed in the last few hundred years or so before the world blew up, but they could have put the Trees around level ground just as well."

"Place of Going to the Stars or not," said Rollo, "there is something here, something protected by the Trees."

"Yes, I suppose you're right. But it was the Place of Stars I wanted."

"The thing that bothers me is why they passed us through. The Trees, I mean. They could have kept us out. The rocks were out there waiting. All the Trees would have had to do was give the word, and the rocks would have moved in and flattened us."

"I've wondered, too. But I'm glad they let us in."

"Because they wanted to let us in. Because they decided it was best to let us in. Not just because they could see no harm in us, but because they wanted us, almost as if they had been waiting all these years for us. Cushing, what did they see in us?"

"Damned if I know," said Cushing. "Come on. I'm going back to camp."

Ezra was huddled close to the fire, fast asleep and snoring. Meg sat beside the fire, wrapped in a blanket against the chill of night. Andy stood a little distance off, hip-shot, head drooping, slack-kneed. Across the fire from Meg, Elayne sat bolt upright, feet tucked under her, hands folded in her lap, her face a blank, eyes fixed on nothing.

"So you're back," said Meg. "See anything, laddie boy?"

"Not a thing," said Cushing. He sat down beside her.

"Hungry? I could cook a slice of venison. Might as well eat it while we can. Another day and it won't be fit to eat."

"I'll get something tomorrow," said Cushing. "There must be deer about."

"I saw a small herd in a break to the west," said Rollo.

"Do you want me to cook up a slice?" asked Meg.

Cushing shook his head. "I'm not hungry."

"Tomorrow we'll climb the hill. You have any idea what we'll find up there?"

"The wardens said there are buildings," Rollo said. "Where the Sleepers sleep."

"We can forget about the Sleepers," Cushing told him. "It's an old wives' tale."

"The wardens built their life upon it," said Rollo. "You'd think it would have to be more than that. Some slight evidence."

"Entire bodies of religion have been built on less," said Cushing.

He picked up a stick of firewood, leaned forward to push the brands of the campfire together. The blaze flared up momentarily and the flare of its light flashed on something that hung in the air just beyond the fire and a short distance above their heads. Cushing reared back in astonishment, the stick of firewood still clutched in his fist.

The thing was cylindrical, three feet long, a foot and a half thick, a fat, stubby torpedo hanging in the air, hanging effortlessly, without wobbling, without any sound, with no ticking or humming that might indicate a mechanism designed to hold it in its place. Along its entire surface, not placed at regular intervals but scattered here and there, were what seemed to be little crystal eyes that glittered in the feeble firelight. The cylinder itself was metal, or seemed to be metal: it had a dull metallic sheen except for the brilliance of the shining eye spots.

"Rollo," said Cushing, "it's a relative of yours."

"I agree," said Rollo, "that it has a robotic look about it, but cross my heart and hope to die, I've never seen one like it."

And here they were, thought Cushing, sitting here and talking about it, being matter-of-fact about it, while by any rule of commonsense they should be frozen stiff with fear. Although, outrageous as it might be, there was no fearsomeness in it, no menace nor any hint of menace, just a fat, roly-poly clown hanging in the air. Looking at it, for a moment he seemed to conjure up a face, a fatuous, vacantly grinning, impish face that was there one moment, gone the next. There never had been any face, he knew; the face that he had seen was the kind of face that should go with the tubby cylinder suspended in the air.

Ezra mumbled in his sleep, gulping, and turned over, then went back to snoring. Elayne sat stark upright; she had not seen the cylinder, or, seeing it, had not deigned to notice it.

"Can you sense it, Meg?" asked Cushing.

"A nothingness, laddie boy," she said, "a cluttered nothingness, disorderly, chaotic, uncertain of itself, friendly, eager, like a homeless dog looking for a home. . . ."

"Human?"

"What do you mean, human? It's not human."

"Human. Like us. Not alien. Not strange."

It spoke to them, its words clipped, metallic. There were no moving mouth parts, no indication of where the words came from;—but there was no doubt that it was the tubby hanger-in-the-air that spoke to them.

"There was a purple liquid," it said. "Not water. Liquid. Heavier than water. Thicker than water. It lay in hollows and then it humped up and flowed across the land. It was a scarlet, sandy land and strange things grew in the scarlet land, barrel-like things and tublike things and ball-like things, but big. Many times bigger than myself. With spines and needles in them that they could see and smell and hear with. And talk, but I can't remember what they said. There is so much that I cannot remember, that I knew at one time and no longer know. They welcomed the purple liquid that rolled across the land, uphill and downhill—it could go anywhere. It rolled in long waves across the scarlet sand and the barrel-like things and the other things welcomed it with song. Thanksgiving, glad the purple came. Although, why glad, I do not remember. It is hard to think why they should welcome it, for when it passed over living things, they died. Their spines and needles all hung limp and they could no longer talk and they caved in upon themselves and lay stinking in the sun. There was a great red sun that filled half the sky and one could look straight into it, for it was not a hot sun, not a bright sun. The purple flowed across the land, then rested in hollows and the barrel-things and the other things it had not yet passed over sang softly to it, inviting it to come. . . ."

Another voice said, louder than the first, trying to blot out the other, "The stars went round and round, the green star and the blue star, and they moved so fast they were not balls of fire but streaks of fire, and rising in that point in space they circled was a cloud that was alive, taking its energy from the two revolving stars, and I wondered if the stars had been this way always or if the cloud that looked to be all sparkle had made the suns go round and round, the cloud telling the two suns what to do and . . ."

And yet another voice: "Darkness, and in the darkness a seething that lived upon the darkness and could not abide the light, that took the feeble light I threw at it and ate it, draining the batteries so there was no longer any light, so that I, powerless, fell into the darkness and the seething closed upon me. . . ."

Still another voice: "A purpleness that entrapped me, that took me in and held me and made me a part of it and told me things of long ago, before the universe began. . . ."

"My God," screamed Meg, "they are all around us!"

And they were. The air seemed full of them, a flock of tubby cylinders that hung above them in the firelight and beyond the firelight, all of them jabbering, each trying to outdo the others.

". . . I could not talk with them, there was no way to talk with them; they did not think or act or see or hear or feel like me; there was nothing that I had that they had, nothing they had I had. . . . It had one body only, a hideous, terrible body that I cannot describe because my senses and my mind rejected the very horridness of it, that I could not describe even had I not rejected it; but one thing I knew, that it had many minds and these minds conversed with one another and they all talked at me and held me in great pity that I had but one mind. . . . They were machines but not machines as we are machines, as I am a machine; they were living metals and sentient plastics and they had a spirit that . . . I was an ant and they did not notice me, they had no idea I was there and I lay there in my antdom and listened to them, experiencing some of what they experienced, not all of it, by any means, for I did not have the knowledge nor the perceptions; like gods they were, and I as dust beneath their feet, although I do not know if they had feet, and I loved them and was terrified by them, both at once. . . . There was this cancer that spread from world to world, that ate everything it touched, and a voice came out of it and told me, 'Behold us, we are life.' . . . There was a people; I don't know if I should call them people, but they had all the time there was, creatures to which time meant nothing, for they had conquered time, or maybe only understood it, and had no longer any fear of its tyranny; and they were miserable, for having obliterated it, they had found that they needed time and had tried to get it back, but could not since they had murdered it. . . . 'I am an exterminator,' it told me. 'I wipe out life that has no right to be; I wipe clean the worlds that got started wrong, that had no right to be. What would you think if I exterminated you?' . . . There was this race of laughers, laughing in their minds; all they could do was laugh, it was their one reaction to anything at all, although it was a different kind of laughter than I had ever known and there was really not that much for them to laugh about. . . ."

Babble, babble, babble. Jabber, jabber, jabber. Clatter, clatter, clatter. Disjointed and fragmentary, although if one of them could have been listened to alone, perhaps the story that it told might be comprehensible. But this was impossible—each with its own story to tell insisted on talking while the others talked so that all of them were talking all at once.

By now there were so many of them and the chatter of them so insistent and intermingled that there was no way of hearing anything except an occasional phrase. Cushing found himself unconsciously hunching his shoulders and tucking in his head, hunkering lower to the ground, assuming a protective stance, as if the increasing babble were an actual physical attack.

Ezra tossed in his sleep and sat up, dazed, scrubbing at his eyes with his fists. His mouth moved, but there was so much babble, there were so many other voices, that he could not be heard.

Cushing turned his head to look at Elayne. She sat as she had before, staring out into the night with the sense of seeing nothing. Ezra had said of her, that first day they had stumbled on the two of them, "She is of another world," and that, Cushing thought, must be the explanation—that she dwelt in two worlds, of which this one, perhaps, was the least important.

Rollo stood on the other side of the fire and there was something wrong about him. Cushing wondered what it was and suddenly he knew: Rollo was alone; Shivering Snake was no longer with him. Thinking back, he tried to recall when he had last seen the snake, and could not be sure.

We are here, Cushing told himself, we are finally here—wherever here might be. Denied access by the wardens, herded by the rocks, let in by the Trees. But before the Trees had let them in, there had been a questioning and a probing, an inquisition, a looking for heresy or sin. Although not probing all of them, perhaps; perhaps only a probing of himself. Certainly not of Meg, for she had helped him when his legs were water and his senses scattered. Not of Ezra, for he had claimed he held a conversation with the Trees. And of Elayne? Of Elayne, who would know? She was a secret person, an exclusive person who shared with no one. Andy? he asked himself. What of Andy, the hunter of water, the killer of rattlesnakes, the battler of bears? He chuckled to himself as he thought of Andy.

Had it been himself alone who had been questioned and examined, the surrogate for all the rest of them, the leader answering for all the rest of them? And in the questioning, in the quest of the dirty fingernails that had pulled the essential being of him apart, what had they found? Something, perhaps, that had persuaded the Trees finally to let them through. He wondered vaguely what that something might have been, and could not know, since he could not know himself.

The babbling stopped of a single instant and the tubby cylinders were gone. Somewhere off in the night a chirping cricket could be heard.

Cushing shook himself, his mind still benumbed by the babble. He felt a physical ache, his entire body aching.

"Someone called them off," said Meg. "Something called them home, reproving them, angry at them."

Elayne said, in her textbook voice, "We came into a homeless frontier, a place where we were not welcome, where nothing that lived was welcome, where thought and logic were abhorrent and we were frightened, but we went into this place because the universe lay before us, and if we were to know ourselves, we must know the universe. . . ."

19

They stopped for their noon rest at the edge of a small grove of trees. Cushing had bagged a deer, which Andy had carried up the slope. Now Cushing and Rollo butchered it and they had their fill of meat.

The going had been hard, uphill all the way, the climb broken by jutting ledges of rocks they had to work their way around, gashed by gullies that time after time forced them to change their course. The dried grass was slippery, making the footing uncertain, and there had been many falls.

Below them the Trees were a dark band of foliage that followed the course of the lower reaches of the butte. Beyond the Trees the high plain was a blur of brown and deeper shadows, thinning out to a lighter, almost silvery hue as it stretched to the horizon. Using the glasses, Cushing saw that now there were more than wardens out on the plains. He could see at least three separate bands, encamped or going about the process of encampment. And these, he knew, must be tribes, or delegations from tribes, perhaps alerted by the wardens as to what had happened. Why, he wondered, should the tribes be moving in? It might mean that the wardens were not a small society of fanatics, as it had seemed, but had the backing of at least some of the western tribes, or were acting for the tribes. The thought worried him, and he decided, as he put the glasses back in their case, to say nothing of it to the others.

There was as yet no sign of the buildings that had been glimpsed through the glasses several days before and that the wardens had said were there. Ahead of them lay only the everlasting slope that they must climb.

"Maybe before the day is over," Rollo said, "we may be in sight of the buildings."

"I hope so," Meg told him. "My feet are getting sore with all this climbing."

The only signs of life they saw were the herd of deer from which Cushing had made his kill, a few long-eared rabbits, a lone marmot that had whistled at them from its ledge of rock, and an eagle that sailed in circles high against the blueness of the sky. The tubby cylinders had not reappeared.

In the middle of the afternoon, as they were toiling up an unusually steep and treacherously grass-slicked slope, they saw the spheres. There were two of them, looking like iridescent soap bubbles, rolling cautiously down the slope toward them. They were a considerable distance off, and as the little band stopped to watch them, the two spheres came to a halt on a fairly level bench at the top of the slope.

From where he stood, Cushing tried to make out what they were. Judging the distance he was from them, he gained the impression they might stand six feet tall. They seemed smooth and polished, perfectly rounded and with no sense of mass; insubstantial beings—and beings because there seemed in his mind no question that they were alive.

Meg had been looking at them through the glasses and now she took them from her face.

"They have eyes," she said. "Floating eyes. Or, at least, they look like eyes and they float all about the surface."

She held out the glasses to him, but he shook his head. "Let's go up," he said, "and find out what they are."

The spheres waited for them as they climbed. When they reached the bench on which the spheres rested, they found themselves no more than twenty feet from their visitors.

As Meg had said, the spheres were possessed of eyes that were scattered all about their surfaces, moving from time to time to new positions.

Cushing walked toward them, with Meg close beside him, the others staying in the rear. The spheres, Cushing saw, were about the size that he had estimated. Except for the eyes, they seemed to have no other organs that were visible.

Six feet from them, Cushing and Meg halted, and for a moment nothing happened. Then one of the spheres made a sound that was a cross between a rumble and a hum. Curiously, it sounded as if the sphere had cleared its throat.

The sphere rumbled once again and this time the rumble defined itself into booming speech. The words were the kind that a drum would make had a drum been able to put together words.

"You are humans, are you not?" it asked. "By humans, we mean—"

"I know what you mean," said Cushing. "Yes, we are human beings."

"You are the intelligent species that is native to this planet?"

"That is right," said Cushing.

"You are the dominant life form?"

"That's correct," said Cushing.

"Then allow me," said the sphere, "to introduce ourselves.

147

Clifford D. Simak

We are a team of investigators who come from many light years
distant. I am Number One and this one that stands beside me is
termed Number Two. Not that one of us is first or the other
second, but simply to give us both identity."

"Well, that is fine," said Cushing, "and we are pleased to
meet you. But would you mind telling me what you are
investigating."

"Not at all," said #1. "In fact, we'd be most happy to, for we
have some hope that you may be able to shed light upon some
questions that puzzle us exceedingly. Our field of study is the
technological civilizations, none of which seem to be viable for
any length of time. They carry within themselves the seeds of
their destruction. On other planets we have visited where
technology has failed, that seems to have been the end of it.
The technology fails and the race that had devised and lived by
it then fails as well. It goes down to barbarism and it does not
rise again, and on the face of it that has happened here. For
more than a thousand years the humans of this planet have
lived in barbarism and give all signs that they will so continue,
but the A and R assures us that it is not so, that the race has
failed time and time again and after a certain period of rest and
recuperation has risen to even greater heights. As so, says the
A and R, will be the pattern of this failure. . . ."

"You are talking riddles," said Cushing. "Who is this A and
R?"

"Why, he is the Ancient and Revered, the A and R for short.
He is a robot and a gentleman and—"

"We have with us a robot," Cushing said. "Rollo, please step
forward and meet these new friends of ours. Our company also
includes a horse."

"We know of horses," said #2 in a deprecatory tone. "They
are animals. But we did not know—"

"Andy is no animal," Meg said acidly. "He may be a horse,

148

but he is a fey horse. He is a searcher-out of water and a battler of bears and many other things besides."

"What I meant to say," said #2, "is that we did not know there were any robots other than the ones that live upon this geographic eminence. We understood that all other robots had been destroyed in your so-called Time of Trouble."

"I am, so far as I am aware," said Rollo, "the only robot left alive. And yet, you say the Ancient and Revered—"

"The Ancient and Revered," said #1, "and a host of others. Surely you have met them. Nasty little creatures that descend upon one and regale one with endless, senseless chatter, all talking at the same time, all insistent that one listen." He sighed. "They are most annoying. For years we have tried to listen to them, in the hope they would provide a clue. But they provide us nothing but a great confusion. I have the theory, not shared by the other member of the Team, they are naught but ancient storytellers who are so programmed that they recite their fictional adventures to anyone they may chance upon, without regard as to whether what they have to tell—"

"Now, wait a minute," said Rollo. "You're sure these things are robots? We had thought so, but I had a hope—"

"You have met them, then?"

"Indeed we have," said Meg. "So you think the things they tell us are no more than tales designed for entertainment?"

"That's what I think," said #1. "The other member of the Team believes, mistakenly, that they may talk significances which we, in our alien stupidity, are not able to understand. Let me ask you, in all honesty, how did they sound to you? As humans you may have been able to see in them something we have missed."

"We listened to them for too short a time," said Cushing, "to arrive at any judgment."

"They were with us for only a short while," said Meg, "then someone called them off."

"The A and R, most likely," said #1. "He keeps a sharp eye on them."

"The A and R—" asked Cushing, "how do we go about meeting him?"

"He is somewhat hard to meet," said #2. "He keeps strictly to himself. On occasion he has granted us audiences."

"Audiences," said #1. "For all the good it did."

"Then he tells you little?"

"He tells us much," said #1, "but of such things as his faith in the human race. He pretends to take an extremely long-range view, and, to be fair about it, he does not seem perturbed."

"You say he is a robot?"

"A robot, undoubtedly," said #2, "but something more than that. As if the robotic part of him is no more than a surface indication of another factor that is much greater."

"That is what you think," said #1. "He is clever, that is all. A very clever robot."

"We should have told you sooner," said #2, "but we tell you now. We are very glad to meet you. No other humans come. We understand the Trees will not let them through. How did you manage to get through the Trees?"

"It was no sweat," said Cushing. "We just asked them and they let us through."

"Then you must be very special persons."

"Not at all," said Meg. "We simply seek the Place of Going to the Stars."

"The going to the what? Did we hear you rightly?"

"The stars," said Meg. "The Place of Going to the Stars."

"But this is not," said #1, "a Place of Going to the Stars. In all the time we've been here, there has been no mention of going to the stars. We know, of course, that one time men went into space, but whether to the stars—"

"You are sure," asked Cushing, "that this is not the Place of Going to the Stars?"

"We have heard no mention of it," said #2. "There is no evidence it was ever used as such. We have the impression that this is the last place of refuge for those elite intellectuals who may have foreseen the Time of Trouble and sought to save themselves. But if this is so, there is no record of it. We do not know; we simply have surmised. The last stronghold of reason on this planet. Although, if that is true, the refuge failed, for there is no indication there have been any humans here for many centuries."

Cushing said, "Not the Place of Going to the Stars?"

"I fear not," said #1.

Rollo said to Cushing, "I never guaranteed it. I simply told you what I heard."

"You said a while ago," said Meg, "that we are the first people ever to come here, implying that you are glad we have. But if you had wanted to meet and talk with people, it would have been quite simple. All you had to do was go and find them. Unless, of course, the Trees would not let you out."

"We did go and seek out people many years ago," said #2. "The Trees are no barrier to us. We can elevate ourselves and sail over them quite easily. But the people would have none of us—they were frightened of us. They ran howling from us or, in desperation, launched attacks upon us."

"And now that we are here," said Cushing, "now that humans have come to you rather than you going to the humans, what can we do for you?"

"You can tell us," said #1, "if there is any basis for the hope and faith expressed so blindly by the A and R that your race will rise to greatness once again."

"Greatness," said Cushing. "I don't know. How do you measure greatness? What is the greatness? Perhaps you can tell me. You say you have studied other planets where technology has failed."

"They all have been the same as this," said #2. "This planet is a classic example of a classic situation. The technological civilization fails and those intelligences that have brought it about go down to nothingness and never rise again."

"Then why does the rule not apply here? What are you worrying about?"

"It's the A and R," said #1. "He insists upon his faith. . . ."

"Has it occurred to you that A and R may be pulling your leg?"

"Pulling our—?"

"Misleading you. Covering up. Perhaps laughing at you."

"It hasn't occurred to us," said #2. "The A and R is very much a gentleman. He'd not do such a thing. You must realize that we have spent millennia collecting our data. This is the first time that data has ever been in question, the only time there has been any doubt at all. All the other studies checked out in every detail. Here you can see our great concern."

"I suppose I can," said Cushing. "Let me ask you this—have you ever gone further than your data, your immediate data? You say you are convinced that when technology fails, the race is done, that there is no coming back. But what happens next? What happens after that? If, on this planet, man sinks into insignificance, what takes his place? What comes after man? What supersedes man?"

"This," said #1, in a stricken tone, "we have never thought about. No one has ever raised the question. We have not raised the question. It had not occurred to us."

The two of them rested for a time, no longer talking, but jiggling back and forth, as if in agitation. Finally #2 said,

"We'll have to think about it. We must study your suggestion."

With that, they started rolling up the slope, their eyes skittering all about their surfaces as they rolled, gathering speed as they went up the slope, so that it did not take long before they were out of sight.

20

Before nightfall, Cushing and the others reached the approach to the City, a huge stone-paved esplanade that fronted on the massive group of gray-stone buildings. They halted to make the evening camp, with an unspoken reluctance to advance into the City itself, preferring to remain on its edge for a time, perhaps to study it from a distance or to become more accustomed to its actuality.

A dozen stone steps went up to the broad expanse of the esplanade, which stretched for a mile or more before the buildings rose into the air. The broad expanse of stone paving was broken by masonry-enclosed flowerbeds that now contained more weeds than flowers, by fountains that now were nonfunctional, by formal pools that now held drifted dust instead of water, by stone benches where one might sit to rest. In one of the nearby flowerbeds a few straggly rosebushes still survived, bearing faded blossoms, with bedraggled rose petals blown by the wind across the stones.

The City, to all appearances, was deserted. There had been, since the evening before, no sign of the tubby gossipers. The Team was not in evidence. There was nothing but a half dozen twittering, discontented birds that flew about from one patch of desiccated shrubs to another desiccated patch.

Above the City stretched the lonely sky, and from where they stood they could see far out into the misty blueness of the plains.

Cushing gathered wood from some of the dead or dying shrubs and built a fire on one of the paving stones. Meg got out the frying pan and sliced steaks off a haunch of venison. Andy, free of his load, clopped up and down the esplanade, like a soldier doing sentry beat, his hoofs making a dull, plopping sound. Ezra sat down beside the stone flower bed that contained the few straggly roses, assuming a listening attitude. Elayne, this time, did not squat down beside him, but walked out several hundred yards across the esplanade and stood there rigidly, facing the City.

"Where is Rollo?" asked Meg. "I haven't seen him all the afternoon."

"Probably out scouting," said Cushing.

"What would he be scouting for? There's nothing to scout."

"He's got a roving foot," said Cushing. "He's scouted every mile since he joined up with us. It's probably just a habit. Don't worry about him. He'll show up."

She put the steaks into the pan. "Laddie boy, this isn't the place we were looking for, is it? It is something else. You have any idea what it is?"

"No idea," said Cushing, shortly.

"And all this time you have had the heart of you so set on finding the Place of Going to the Stars. It's a crying shame, it is. Where did we go wrong?"

"Maybe," said Cushing, "there is no such place as Going to

the Stars. It may be just a story. There are so many stories."

"I can't think that," said Meg. "Somehow, laddie buck, I just can't think it. There has to be such a place."

"There should be," Cushing told her. "Fifteen hundred years ago or more, men went to the moon and Mars. They wouldn't have stopped with that. They'd have gone farther out. But this is not the right kind of place. They'd have had to have launching pads, and it's ridiculous to build launching pads up here. Up here, it would be difficult to transport the sort of support such a base would need."

"Maybe they found a different way of going to the stars. This might be the place, after all."

Cushing shook his head. "I don't think so."

"But this place is important. It has to be important. Why else would it be guarded by the Trees? Why were the wardens out there?"

"We'll find out," said Cushing. "We'll try to find out."

Meg shivered. "I have a funny feeling in my bones," she said. "As if we shouldn't be here. As if we're out of place. I can feel those big buildings looking down at us, wondering who we are and why we're here. When I look at them, I go all over goose pimples."

A voice said, "Here, let me do that."

Meg looked up. Elayne was bending over her, reaching for the pan.

"That's all right," said Meg. "I can manage it."

"You've been doing it all the time," said Elayne. "Doing all the cooking. I haven't done a thing. Let me do my part."

"All right," said Meg. "Thank you, lass. I'm tired."

She rose from her crouch, moved over to a stone bench and sat down. Cushing sat beside her.

"What was that?" he asked. "What is going on? Can she be getting human?"

"I don't know," said Meg. "But whatever the reason, I'm glad. I'm bone tired. It's been a long, hard trip. Although I wouldn't have missed it for the world. I'm glad we're here, uneasy as I may be about it."

"Don't let the uneasiness get you down," he said. "It will seem different in the morning."

When they came in at Elayne's call to supper, Ezra roused himself from his communion with the roses and joined them. He wagged his head in perplexity. "I do not understand at all," he said, "the things the roses tell me. There is about them a sense of ancientness, of far places, of time for which there is no counting. As if they were trying to push me to the edge of the universe, from which I could look out upon eternity and infinity, and then they ask me what I see and I cannot tell them, because there is too much to see. There are powerful forces here and mysteries that no man can fathom. . . ."

He went on and on, mumbling in a rambling way as he ate the meal. No one interrupted him; no one asked him questions. Cushing found himself not even listening.

Hours later, Cushing woke. The others were asleep. The fire had burned to a few glowing embers. Andy stood a little way off, head hanging, either fast asleep upon his feet or dozing.

Cushing threw aside his blanket and rose to his feet. The night had turned chilly, and overhead the wind made a hollow booming among the brilliant stars. The moon had set, but the buildings were a ghostly white in the feeble starlight.

Moving off, he walked in the direction of the City, stopped to face it, his eyes traveling up the clifflike face of it. I could do without you, he told the City, the words dribbling in his mind. I have no liking for you. I did not set out to find you.

Too big, he thought, too big, wondering if he, in that moment, might be thinking as other men had thought when they struck the blow that had toppled that great, impersonal technology that had engulfed and overwhelmed them.

Striking, they had toppled a way of life that had become abhorrent to them, but instead of replacing it with another way of life, they had left an emptiness, a vacuum in which it was impossible to exist, retreating back to an older existence, back almost to where they'd started, as a man might go back to old roots to seek a new beginning. But they had made no beginning; they had simply stood in place, perhaps content for a while to lick their wounds and rest, to catch their breath again. They had caught their breath and rested and the wounds had healed and they still had stood in place—for centuries they had not moved. Perhaps fearful of moving, fearful that if they moved, they would create another monster that in time to come they'd also have to destroy, asking themselves how many false starts a race might be allowed.

Although, he knew, he was romanticizing, philosophizing on insufficient grounds. The trouble had been that the people after the Collapse had not thought at all. Bruised and battered after all the years of progress, they had simply huddled, and were huddling still.

And this great building—or perhaps many buildings, each masking the other, so that there seemed but one building— what could it be, standing here in a place that was a wilderness and had always been a wilderness? A special structure, built for a specific reason, perhaps a mysterious and secretive reason, guarded as it was by the Trees and the living stones? So far, there was no clue as to what might be the reason. Nor a clue to the Trees and stones. And none, for that matter, to the Followers and to Shivering Snake.

He walked slowly across the esplanade toward the City. Directly ahead of him rose two great towers, square-built and solid, endowed with no architectural foolishness, guarding a darkness that could be either a shadow or a door.

As he drew closer, he could see that it was a door and that it was open. A short and shallow flight of stone stairs led up to the door, and as he began to climb them, he saw a flash of light in the darkness that lay beyond the door. He halted and stood breathless, watching, but the flash was not repeated.

The door was larger than he'd thought, twenty feet wide or more, and rising to a height of forty feet or so. It opened into a place of darkness. Reaching it, he stood undecided for a moment, then moved through it, shuffling his feet to guard against any drop or irregularity in the floor.

A few feet inside, he stopped again and waited for his eyes to adapt, but the darkness was so deep that little adaptation was possible. The best that he could do was make out certain graduations in the darkness, the darker loom of objects that stood along the walls of the corridor through which he moved.

Then, ahead of him, a light flashed, and then another, and after that many flashes of light, strange, quivering, looping lights that sparkled rather than shone, and, after a moment of near panic, he knew what they were: hundreds of shivering snakes, dancing in the darkness of a room that opened off the corridor.

Heart halfway up his throat, he headed for the door and reached it. Standing in it, neither in nor out, he could see the room, or half see it, a place of large dimensions with a massive table set in the middle of it, the room lighted in a flickering manner by the zany loopings of the zany snakes; and standing at the head of the table, a form that did not seem to be a man, but a form that was suggestive of a man.

Cushing tried to speak, but the words dried up before he

could get them out and shattered into a dust that seemed to coat his mouth and throat, and when he tried to speak again, he found that he could not remember what he had meant to say, and even if he had been able to, he could not have spoken.

A soft hand touched his arm and Elayne's voice sounded. "Here we stand on the edge of eternity," she said. "One step and we'll be into eternity and it would reveal itself to us. Cannot you feel it?"

He shook his head abjectly. He was feeling nothing except a terrible numbness that so paralyzed him he doubted he would ever be able to move from the spot where he was rooted.

He was able, with an effort, to turn his head slightly to one side, and he saw her standing there beside him, slim and straight in the tattered, smudged robe that once had been white, but was no longer. In the flicker of the snakes her face and its emptiness were more terrible than he had ever seen it, a frightening, soul-withering face, but his basic numbness precluded further fright and he looked upon the face without a quiver of emotion, simply noting to himself the utter horror of it.

Her voice, however, was clear and precise. There was no emotion in it, not a tremor, as she said, "As my grandfather told us, as the plants had told him, eternity is here. It lies within our grasp. It is just beyond our fingertips. It is a strange condition, unlike the eternity we have thought about—a place with neither time nor space, for there is not room in it for either time or space. It is an all-encompassing endlessness that never had a beginning and will not have an end. Embedded in it are all those things that have happened or are about to happen. . . ." Then she gasped and her grip on Cushing's arm tightened until he could feel her nails cutting deep into his flesh. She sobbed, "It's not like that at all. That was only superficial. It is a place—no, not a place. . ." She sagged and Cushing caught her as she slumped, holding her upright.

The figure at the head of the table stood unmoving. Cushing looked at it across the intervening space and it looked back at him out of gleaming eyes that sparkled in the dazzle of the light supplied by the spinning, twisting snakes.

Elayne sagged, her legs buckling under her. Cushing swept her up in his arms and turned about, heading for the door. He felt the eyes of the figure at the table's head burning into him, but he did not turn his head. He stumbled out the door and down the corridor until he had passed through the outer door and down the steps onto the esplanade. There he stopped and let Elayne down, and her knees did not buckle under her. She stood erect, clinging to him for support. In the pale starlight, her vacant face held a stricken look.

Off to one side came a clatter of hoofs, and switching his head about, Cushing saw that it was Andy, prancing and gamboling in a mad abandon, neck bowed, tail straight out behind him, dancing on the paving stones. For a moment it seemed that he was alone; then Cushing saw the others—faint shadows in the starlight, running madly with him like a pack of joyous wolves, circling him and leaping over him, running underneath his belly, leaping up playfully to confront him and fawn on him, as a pack of puppies might play with a delightedly shrieking four-year-old.

Elayne jerked away from him and began to run, back toward the camp, running silently, robe fluttering behind her. Cushing pounded after her, but she outdistanced him. Meg rose up from the camp and confronted her, grappling with her to halt the frenzied flight.

161

"What's the matter with her, laddie boy?" asked Meg as he came up. "What have you done to her?"

"Not a thing," said Cushing. "She just saw reality, is all. We were inside the City and she was delivering some of that insipid nonsense, mostly about eternity, she has been spouting all the time, and then—"

"You were in the City?"

"Yes, of course," said Cushing. "They left the door wide open."

Elayne had sunk to her ritual position, feet tucked under her, hands folded in her lap, head bowed. Ezra, fumbling out of his blanket, was fussing over her.

"What did you find in there?" asked Meg. "And what has got into Andy?"

"He's dancing with a gaggle of Followers," said Cushing. "Never mind about him. He's making out all right."

"And Rollo? Where is Rollo?"

"Damned if I know," said Cushing. "He is never here when we have need of him. Just ambling about."

A cylinder appeared in the air above them, hanging motionless, its receptors gleaming at them.

"Go away," said Cushing. "Right now, we don't need another story."

"No story have I to tell you," said the gossiper. "I carry information for you. I have a message from the A and R."

"The A and R?"

"The Ancient and Revered. He said for me to tell you that the City is closed to you. He said to say we have no time to waste on a group of gaping tourists."

"Well, that's all right," said Meg. "We aren't gaping tourists, but we'll be glad to leave."

"That you cannot do," said the gossiper. "That will not be

allowed. You are not to leave; for if you do, you will carry foolish tales with you, and that we do not want."

"So," said Cushing, "we are not allowed to leave and the City is closed to us. What do you expect us to do?"

"That is up to you," said the gossiper. "It is no concern of ours."

21

Three days later they knew that what the gossiper had said was true. Meg and Cushing had toured the City, looking for a means of getting into it. They found none. There were doors, a lot of doors, but all were closed and locked. The windows, and there were few of them, were no lower than the second or third floors. The few they were able to reach were locked as well and constructed of something other than glass, impossible to break. What was more, they were opaque and there was no way of looking through them. Ventilating shafts, of which there were only a few, were baffled in such a manner that they offered no opportunity of crawling through them.

The City was much larger than it had appeared, and it was, they found, a single building with many wings; in fact, with wings added on to wings, so the scheme of construction, at times, became confusing. The heights of the divers wings varied, some only five or six stories tall, others rising to twenty stories or more. The entire structure was flanked all the way around by the stone-paved esplanade.

Except for one occasion, on the second day, they saw no one. On that second day, late in the afternoon, they had come upon the Team, apparently waiting for them when they came around the corner of one of the many wings.

Meg and Cushing stopped in astonishment, yet somewhat glad at meeting something with which they could communicate. The two great globes rolled forward to meet them, their eyes floating randomly. When they reached one of the stone benches, they stopped to wait for the humans to come up.

#1 boomed at them in his drumlike voice. "Please to sit down and rest yourselves, as we note is the custom of your kind. Then it will be possible to have communication very much at leisure."

"We have been wondering," Meg said, "what had happened to you. That day we talked, you left in something of a hurry."

"We have been cogitating," said #2, "and very much disturbed by the thing you told us—the question that you asked."

"You mean," said Cushing, "What comes after man?"

"That is it," said #1, "and it was not the concept that was so disturbing to us, but that it could be asked of any race about itself. This is much at odds with the viewpoint of the A and R, who seems quite convinced that your race will recover from the late catastrophe and rise again to greater heights than you have ever known before. By any chance, have you met the A and R?"

"No," Cushing said, "we haven't."

"Ah, then," said #2, "to return to the question that you asked. Can you explain to us how you came to ask it? To say of something else that in time it will be superseded by some other form of life is only logical, but for a species to entertain the idea

165

that it will be superseded argues a sophistication that we had not considered possible."

"To answer that one," said Cushing, "is really very simple. Such a speculation is only commonsense and is quite in line with evolutionary mechanics. Life forms rise to dominance because of certain survival factors. On this planet, through the ages, there have been many dominant races. Man rose to his dominance because of intelligence, but geological history argues that he will not remain dominant forever. And once that is recognized, the question naturally rises as to what will come after him. What, we might ask, has a greater survival value than intelligence? And though we cannot answer, we know there must be something. As a matter of fact, it might seem that intelligence has turned out to have poor survival value."

"And you do not protest?" asked #2. "You do not pound your chest in anger? You do not tear your hair? You do not grow weak and panicky at the thought the day will come when there will be none of you, that in the universe there will be nothing like you, that there will be none to remember or to mourn you?"

"Hell, no," said Cushing. "No, of course we don't."

"You can so disregard your own personal reactions," said #2, "as to actually speculate upon what will follow you?"

"I think," said Meg, "it might be fun to know."

"We fail to comprehend," said #1. "This fun you speak about. What do you mean by 'fun'?"

"You mean, poor things," cried Meg, "that you never have any fun? That you don't know what we mean by 'fun'?"

"We catch the concept barely," said #2, "although perhaps imperfectly. It is something we have not heretofore encountered. We find it hard to understand that any being could derive even the slightest satisfaction in regarding its own extinction."

"Well," said Cushing, "we aren't extinct as yet. We may have a few more years."

"But you don't do anything about it."

"Not actively," said Cushing. "Not now. Perhaps not at any time. We just try to get along. But, now, suppose you tell us—do you have even an inkling of an answer to the question that we asked? What does come after us?"

"It's a question we can't answer," said #1, "although since you spoke of it to us, we have given thought to it. The A and R contends that the race will continue. But we think the A and R is wrong. We have seen other planets where the dominant races have fallen and that was the end of it. There was nothing that gave promise of coming after them."

"Perhaps," said Cushing, "you weren't able to hang around long enough. It might take some time for another form of life to move in, to fill the vacuum."

"We don't know about that," said #2. "It was something that did not greatly concern us; it was a factor, actually, that we never once considered. It fell outside the area of our study. You understand, the two of us have spent a lifetime on the study of certain crisis points resulting in the terminations of technological societies. On many other planets we have found a classic pattern. The technology builds up to a certain point and then destroys itself and the race that built it. We were about to return to our home planet and inscribe our report when we happened on this planet and the doubt crept in. . . ."

"The doubt crept in," said #1, "because of the evasiveness and the stubbornness of the A and R. He refuses to admit the obvious. He pretends, sometimes convincingly, to hold fast to the faith that your human race will rise again, that it is unconquerable, that it has a built-in spirit that will not accept defeat. He talks obliquely about what he calls a phoenix rising from its ashes, an allusion that escapes us in its entirety."

167

"There is no need to beat among the bushes," said #2. "It seems to us you may be able to abstract an answer more readily than we, and it is our hope that once you have it, you would, in all friendliness, be pleased to share it with us. It seems to us the answer, if there is one, which we doubt exceedingly, is locked within this City. As natives of this planet, you might have a better chance of finding it than we, who are travel-worn aliens, battered by our doubts and inadequacies."

"Fat chance," said Cushing. "We are locked out of the City and, supposedly, marooned here. We are forbidden by the A and R to leave."

"We thought you had said you had not seen the A and R."

"We haven't. He sent a message to us by one of his gossipers."

"The nasty little thing was malicious about it," Meg told them.

"That sounds like the A and R," said #1. "A sophisticated old gentleman, but at times a testy one."

"A gentleman, you say? Could the A and R be human?"

"No, of course he's not," said #2. "We told you. He's a robot. You must know of robots. There is one who is a member of your party."

"Now, wait a minute," said Cushing. "There was something standing at the table's head. It looked like a man and yet not like a man. It could have been a robot. It could have been the A and R."

"Did you speak to it?"

"No, I did not speak to it. There were too many other things. . . ."

"You should have spoken to it."

"Dammit, I know I should have spoken to it, but I didn't. Now it is too late. The A and R is inside the City and we can't get to him."

"It's not only the A and R," said #1. "There is something else shut up behind those walls. We know not directly of it. We but suspicion it. We have only recepted it."

"You mean that you have sensed it."

"That is right," said #1. "Our feeling of it is most unreliable, but it is all that we can tell you."

Cushing and Meg went back at the end of the day to the deserted camp. A little later, Andy came ambling in to greet them. There was no sign of the other three. Ezra and Elayne had gone down the butte to talk with the Trees, and Rollo had simply wandered off.

"We know now, laddie buck," said Meg. "The A and R meant exactly what he said. The City's closed to us."

"It was that damn Elayne," said Cushing. "She was gushing this eternity stuff that she has a hangup on. . . ."

"You're too harsh with her," said Meg. "Her brain may be a little addled, but she has a certain power. I am sure she has. She lives in another world, on another level. She sees and hears things we do not see and hear. And anyhow, it does no good to talk about it now. What are we going to do if we can't get off this butte?"

"I'm not ready to give up yet," said Cushing. "If we want to get out of here, we'll find a way."

"Whatever happened to the Place of Stars," she asked, "that we started out to find? How did we go wrong?"

"We went wrong," said Cushing, "because we were going blind. We grabbed at every rumor that we heard, at all the campfire stories that Rollo had picked up. It wasn't Rollo's fault. It was mine. I was too anxious. I was too ready to accept anything I heard."

Rollo came in shortly after dark. He squatted down beside the other two and sat staring at the fire.

"I didn't find much," he said. "I found a quarry over to the west, where the rock was quarried for the City. I found an old road that led off to the southwest, built and used before the Trees were planted. Now the Trees close off the road. I tried to get through them and there was no getting through. I tried in several places. They simply build a wall against you. Maybe a hundred men with axes could get through, but we haven't got a hundred men with axes."

"Even with axes," said Meg, "I doubt we would get through."

"The tribes are gathering," said Rollo. "The plains off to the east and south are simply black with them, and more coming all the time. The word must have traveled fast."

"What I can't understand," said Cushing, "is why they should be gathering. There were the wardens, of course, but I thought they were just a few small bands of deluded fanatics."

"Perhaps not so deluded," said Meg. "You don't keep a watch for centuries out of pure delusion."

"You think this place is important? That important?"

"It has to be," said Meg. "It is so big. It took so much work and time to build it. And it's so well protected. Men, even men in the old machine days, would not have spent so much time and effort. . . ."

"Yes, I know," said Cushing. "I wonder what it is. Why it's here. If there were only some way for us to dig out the meaning of it."

"The gathering of the tribes," said Rollo, "argues that it may be more important than we know. It was not just the wardens alone. They were backed by the tribes. Maybe sent here and kept here by the tribes. There may be a legend. . . ."

"If so," said Meg, "a well-guarded legend. I have never heard of it. The city tribes back home, I'm sure, never heard of it."

"The best legends," said Cushing, "might be the best

guarded. So sacred, perhaps, that no one ever spoke aloud of them."

The next day, Rollo went with them for another tour of the City. They found nothing new. The walls stood up straight and inscrutable. There was no indication of any life.

Late in the afternoon, Ezra and Elayne returned to camp. They came in footsore and limping, clearly worn out.

"Here, sit down," said Meg, "and rest yourselves. Lie down if you want to. We have water and I'll cook some meat. If you want to sleep a while before you eat . . ."

Ezra croaked at them, "The Trees would not let us through. No argument can budge them. They will not tell us why. But they would talk of other things. They talked of ancestral memories, their ancestral memories. On another planet, in some other solar system, very far from here. They had a name for it, but it was a complicated name with many syllables, and I failed to catch it and did not want to ask again, for it seemed of no importance. Even if we knew the name, it would be of no use to us. They either had forgotten how they got here or did not want to tell us, although I think they may not know. I'm not sure they ever saw the planet that they talked of. They were talking, I think, of ancestral memories. Racial memories, carried forward from one generation to the next."

"You are certain of this?" asked Cushing. "Their saying they came from another planet?"

"I am very certain," Ezra said. "There is no question of it. They talked to me of the planet, as a man marooned in some strange place would talk about the country of his boyhood. They showed the planet to me—admittedly, a very fuzzy picture, but one could recognize certain features of it. An idealized picture, I am certain. I think of it as a pink world— you know, the delicate pink of apple blossoms in the early spring, blowing on a hill against a deep-blue sky. Not only was

171

the *color* of the world pink, but the *feel* of it. I know I'm not telling this too well, but that's how it seemed to me. A glad world—not a happy world, but a glad world."

"Could it be?" asked Cushing. "Could it be that men did go to the stars, to this pink world, bringing back with them the seeds of the Trees?"

"And," said Meg, "the Followers and the Shivering Snakes? The living stones as well? For these things cannot be of this world of ours. There is no way they could be natives of this world."

"And if all of this is true," said Rollo, "then this, after all, may be the Place of Going to the Stars."

Cushing shook his head. "There are no launching pads. We would have found them if there had been any. And so remote, so far from all the sources of supply. The economics of such a place as this would be illogical."

"Perhaps," said Rollo, "a certain amount of illogic could make a certain sense."

"Not in a technological world," said Cushing. "Not in the kind of world that sent men to the stars."

That night, after Ezra and Elayne were sound asleep, Rollo disappeared on another walkabout, and with Andy off to gambol with the Followers, Cushing said to Meg, "One thing keeps bothering me. Something that the Team told us. There is something else here, they said. Something other than the A and R. Something hidden, something we should find."

Meg nodded. "Perhaps, laddie boy," she said. "Perhaps there's a deal to find. But how do we go about it? Has that driving, adventurous brain of yours come up with a fresh idea?"

"You sensed the living rock," said Cushing, "that night long ago. You sensed the Followers. They were a crowd, you said. A conglomerate of many different people, all the people they had ever met. You sensed that the robotic brain still lived. Without half trying, you sensed all these things. You knew I was sleeping in the lilac thicket."

"I've told you and told you, time and time again," she said, "that I'm a piss-poor witch. I'm nothing but an old bag who used her feeble talents to keep life within her body and ill-wishers off her back. A dowdy old bitch, vicious and without ethics, who owes you, laddie buck, more than I ever can repay you for taking me on this great adventure."

"Without half trying," said Cushing, "just as a flippant, everyday exercise of your talents. . . ."

"There's Elayne. She's the one you should be—"

"Not Elayne. Her talents are of a different kind. She gets the big picture, the overview. You get down to basics; you can handle detail. You see the nuts and bolts, sense what is taking place."

"Mad you are," she said. "Madder than a hare."

"Will you do it, Meg?"

"It would be a waste of time."

"We've got to crack this puzzle. We have to know what's going on. If we don't want to stay here forever, penned upon this butte."

"Okay. Tomorrow, then. Just to show you you are wrong. If you have the time to waste."

"I have time to waste," said Cushing. "I have nothing more to do with it."

22

She didn't want to do it, but, she told herself, she had to try, if for no other reason than to get it over with. As well, she was afraid to try it, because then she might learn the true smallness of her powers. If she had any powers at all. Although, she told herself, with slim comfort, she had done certain things.

"I hope," she said to Cushing, "that you are satisfied."

The early morning sun lit the great metal doors, embossed with symbolic figures that meant nothing to her. The stone towers that rose on either side and above the doors were forbidding in their solidity. She gained the impression, as she and the others stood there, at the foot of the shallow stone steps that went up to the door, that the entire building was frowning down upon them.

The Team had said that there was something somewhere behind the doors, somewhere in the City, but they had not known what it was and now it was her job to find out. It was an impossible task, she knew, and she would not have even tried, but laddie boy had faith in her and she could not let him down. The others, she knew, had no faith in her, for she had given them no reason. She looked at Elayne and, for a moment, thought she could glimpse in the other woman's eyes a hint of quiet amusement, although, God knows, she told herself, there is none to know what might be in Elayne's vacant eyes.

She dropped to her knees and settled comfortably, her haunches resting on her heels. She tried to make her mind reach out, easily at first, not pushing too hard, driving out, gently, the tendrils of her mind, seeking, probing, as the tendrils of a climbing vine might seek out crevices in the wall on which it climbed. She sensed the hardness of the stone, the polished toughness of the metal, and then was through them, into the emptiness beyond. And there was something there.

The tendrils pulled back as they touched the strangeness of it—a sort of thing (or things) she had never known before, that no one had ever known before. Not a thing, she told herself, but many slippery different things that had no definition. That would not define themselves, she realized, as her mind veered away from them, because they were not alive, or at least seemed to have no life, although there was no doubt that they were entities of some sort. A tingling fear went through her—a shuddering, a loathing—as if there were spiders there, a billion scurrying spiders with swollen, distended bodies, and legs covered with quivering black hairs. A scream welled in her throat, but she choked it back. They can't hurt me, she told herself; they can't reach me; they're in there and I'm out here.

She thrust her mind at them and was in the midst of them, and now that she was there, she knew they weren't spiders, that there was no harm in them, for they were not alive. But despite the fact of their being lifeless, they somehow held a meaning. That was senseless, she knew. How could something lifeless hold a meaning, or many tiny lifeless things hold many,

Clifford D. Simak

many meanings? For she was surrounded and engulfed by the meanings of them, little lifeless meanings that whispered vaguely at her, thrusting themselves forward, pressing themselves against her, seeking her attention. She sensed the countless buzzings of many tiny energies, and within her mind, fleeting images built up momentarily, then faded, fading almost as soon as they had formed—not one of them, but hordes of them, like a swarm of gnats flying in a shaft of sunlight, not really seeing them, but knowing they were there by the glint of light off the vibrations of their wings.

She tried to concentrate, to bring her mental tendrils down to sharper focuses that could spear and hold at least one of the little dancing images, to seize upon and hold it long enough to make out what it was. She felt, as if from far away, as if it were happening to someone other than herself, the sweat upon her forehead and running down her face. She bent even farther forward, squeezing her upper torso down against her thighs, concentrating her body into a smaller space, as if by this concentration she could concentrate her powers. She squeezed her eyes tight shut, trying to block out all light, to form within her mind a black mental screen upon which she could bring into focus one of the shimmering gnats that danced within her head.

The images did seem to sharpen, but they still danced and flitted, the glitter still came off the whirring wings, masking the half forms that she forced them to take, dim and shadowy, with no real definition. It was no use, she thought; she had driven herself as far as she could go and then had failed. There was something there, some subtle strangeness, but she could not grasp it.

She collapsed, pitching forward, rolling over on her side, still compressed into a fetal position. She let her eyes come open and dimly saw Cushing bending over her.

176

She whispered at him. "I'm all right, laddie boy. There is something there, but I could not catch it. I could not sharpen it, bring it into focus."

He knelt beside her and half lifted her, holding her in his arms. "It's all right, Meg," he said. "You did what you could."

"If I'd had my crystal ball," she whispered.

"Your crystal ball?"

"Yes. I had one. I left it back at home. I never did place much faith in it. It was just window dressing."

"You think it would have helped you?"

"Maybe. It would help me concentrate. I had trouble concentrating."

The others stood around, watching the two of them. Andy shuffled in closer, stretching out his long neck to snuffle at Meg. She patted his nose. "He always worries about me," she said. "He thinks it's his job to take care of me."

She pulled herself away from Cushing and sat up.

"Give me a little time," she said. "Then I'll try again."

"You don't have to," Cushing said.

"I have to. The Team was right. There is something there."

The great stone walls rose up against the cloudless sky—stolid, mocking, hostile. High in the blueness a great bird, reduced by distance to a fly-sized speck, appeared to hang motionless.

"Bugs," she said. "A million little bugs. Scurrying. Buzzing. Like ants, like spiders, like gnats. All the time moving. Confused. And so was I. Never so confused."

Elayne spoke in her hard, cold voice. "I could help," she said.

"Dearie, you stay out of this," said Meg. "I have trouble enough without you butting in."

She got to her knees again, settled back so her haunches rested on her heels.

Clifford D. Simak

"This is the last go I have at it," she said. "Absolutely the last. If it doesn't work this time, that's the end of it."

It was easier this time. There was no need of breaking through the stone and metal. Immediately, once again, she was with the spiders and the gnats. And, this time, the gnats flew in patterns, forming symbols that she could glimpse, but never clearly and never with an understanding, although it seemed to her that the understanding was just a hairsbreadth beyond perception. If she could only drive in a little closer, if somehow she could slow the dancing of the gnats or retard the scurry of the spiders, then it seemed to her that she might catch and hold some small bit of understanding. For there must be purpose in them; there must be a reason they flew or scurried as they did. It could not all be random; there must be reason somewhere in the tapestry they wove. She tried to drive in, and for an instant the mad dance of the gnats slowed its tempo, and in that instant she felt the happiness, the sudden rose-glow of happiness so deep and pure that it was a psychic shock, rocking her back on her mental heels, engulfing her in the abandoned sweetness of it. But even as she knew it, she knew as well that it was somehow wrong—that it was immoral, if not illegal, to know so deep a happiness. And in the instant that she thought that, there came to her the knowing of what was wrong with it. It was, she knew instinctively, a manufactured happiness, a synthetic happiness; and her groping, confused mind caught a fleeting image of a complicated set of symbols that might explain the happiness, that might even cause the happiness. All this within so short a span of time that it was scarcely measureable; then the happiness was gone, and despite the synthetic nature of it, the place seemed bleak and cold and hard without it, an emptiness despite the fact that it was still inhabited by a billion billion insects that she knew weren't really insects but only something that her human mind translated into insects. Moaning, she sought for the happiness again; phoney as it might be, it was a thing she needed, with an hysterical desperation, to touch again, to hold it only for a moment, to know the rose-glow of it. She could not continue in the drabness that was the world without it. Moaning piteously, she reached out for it and had it once again, but even as her mind's fingers touched it, the rose-glow slipped away and was gone again.

From far away, from another world, someone spoke to her, a voice that she once had known but could not identify. *"Here, Meg,"* it said, *"here is your crystal ball."*

She felt the hardness and the roundness of the ball placed between her palms, and, opening her eyes a slit, saw the polished brightness of it, shining in the rays of the morning sun.

Another mind exploded and impacted in her mind—a cold, sharp, dark mind that screamed in triumph and relief, as if the thing that it had awaited had finally happened, while at the same time shrinking back in fear against the gross reality of a condition it had not known for centuries piled on centuries, that it had forgotten, that it had lost all hope of regaining and that now it found thrust so forcefully upon it.

The unsuspected mind clung to her mind, fastening upon it as the one security it knew, clinging desperately, afraid of being alone again, of being thrust back into the darkness and the cold. It clung to her mind in frantic desperation. It ran along the projections of her mind into that place where spiders and gnats cavorted. It recoiled for a fraction of a second, then drove in, taking her mind with it, deep into the swarm of glittering wings and frantic hairy legs, and as it did, the wings and legs were gone, the spiders and the gnats were gone, and out of the whirlpool of uncertainty and confusion came an orderliness that was as confusing as the spiders and gnats. An orderliness that was confusing because it was, in most parts, incomprehensible, a marshaling and a sorting of configurations that even in their neatness seemed to have no meaning.

Then the meanings came—half meanings, guessed meanings, shadowy and fragmented, but solid and real in the shadow and the fragments. They piled into her mind, overwhelming it, clogging it, so that she only caught a part of them, as a person listening to a conversation delivered in so rapid-fire a manner that only one word in twenty could be heard. But beyond all this she grasped for a moment the larger context of it, of all of it—a seething mass of knowledge that seemed to fill and overflow the universe, all the questions answered that ever had been asked.

Her mind snapped back, retracting from the overpowering mass of answers, and her eyes came open. The crystal ball fell from her hands and rolled off her lap, to bounce upon the stony pavement. She saw that it was no crystal ball, but the robotic brain case that Rollo had carried in his sack. She reached out and stroked it with her fingers, mumuring at it, soothing it, aghast at what she'd done. To awaken it, to let it know it was not alone, to raise a hope that could not be carried out—that, she told herself, was a cruelty that could never be erased, for which there could be no recompense. To wake it for a moment, then plunge it back again into the loneliness and the dark, to touch it for a moment and then to let it go. She picked it up and cuddled it against her breasts, as a mother might a child.

"You are not alone," she told it. "I'll stay with you." Not knowing, as she spoke the words, if she could or not. In that time of doubt she felt its mind again—no longer cold, no longer alone or dark, a warmth of sudden comradeship, an overflowing of abject gratitude.

Above her the great metal doors were opening. In them stood a robot, a larger and more massive machine than Rollo, but very much akin to him.

"I'm called the Ancient and Revered," the robot told them. "Won't you please come in? I should like to talk with you."

23

They sat at the table in the room where Cushing and Elayne had first met the A and R, but this time there was light from a candle that stood at one end of the table. There were Shivering Snakes as well, but not as many as there had been that first time, and those that were there stayed close against the ceiling, looping and spinning and making damn fools of themselves.

The A and R sat down ponderously in the chair at the table's head and the others of them took chairs and ranged themselves on either side. Meg laid the robot's brain case on the table in front of her and kept both hands upon it, not really holding it but just letting it know that she was there. Every now and then she felt the presence probing gently at her mind, perhaps simply to assure itself that she had not deserted it. Andy stood in the doorway, half in the room, half out, his head drooping but watching everything. Behind him in the corridor fluttered the gray shapes of his pals the Followers.

The A and R settled himself comfortably in the chair and

looked at them for a long time before he spoke, as if he might be evaluating them, perhaps debating with himself the question of whether he might have made a mistake in inviting them to this conference.

Finally, he spoke. "I am pleased," he said, "to welcome you to the Place of Going to the Stars."

Cushing hit the table with his open hand. "Cut out the fairy tales," he yelled. "This can't be the Place of Going to the Stars. There are no launching pads. In a place like this the logistics would be impossible."

"Mr. Cushing," the A and R said gently, "if you'll allow me to explain. No launching pads, you say. Of course there are no launching pads. Have you ever tried to calculate the problems of going to the stars? How far they are, the time that it would take to reach them, the shortness of a human life?"

"I've read the literature," said Cushing. "The library at the university—"

"You read the speculations," said the A and R. "You read what was written about going to the stars centuries before there was any possibility of going to the stars. Written when men had reached no farther into space than the moon and Mars."

"That is right, but—"

"You read about cryogenics: freezing the passengers and then reviving them. You read the controversies about faster-than-light. You read the hopefulness of human colonies planted on the earthlike planets of other solar systems."

"Some of it might have worked," said Cushing stubbornly. "Men, in time, would have found better ways to do it."

"They did," said the A and R. "Some men did go to some of the nearby stars. They found many things that were interesting. They brought back the seeds from which sprouted the belt of Trees that rings in this butte. They brought back the living rocks, the Shivering Snakes and the Followers, all of which you've seen. But it was impractical. It was too costly and the time factor was too great. You speak of logistics, and the logistics of sending human beings to the stars were wrong. Once you get into a technological system, once it's actually in operation, you find what's wrong with it. Your perspectives change and your goals tend to shift about. You ask yourself what you really want, what you're trying to accomplish, what values can be found in the effort you are making. We asked this of ourselves once we started going to the stars and the conclusion was that the actual landing on another planet of another solar system was, in itself, of not too great a value. There was glory, of course, and satisfaction, and we learned some things of value, but the process was too slow; it took too long. If we could have sent out a thousand ships, each pointed toward a different point in space, the returns would have been speeded up. It would have taken as long, but with that many ships there would have been a steady feedback of results, after a wait of a few hundred years, as the ships began coming back, one by one. But we could not send out a thousand ships. The economy would not withstand that sort of strain. And once you had sent out a thousand ships, you'd have to keep on building them and sending them out to keep the pipeline full. We knew we did not have the resources to do anything like that and we knew we didn't have the time, for some of our social scientists were warning us of the Collapse that finally overtook us. So we asked ourselves—we were forced to ask ourselves—what we were really looking for. And the answer seemed to be that we were seeking information.

"Without having lived through the era of which I talk, it is difficult to comprehend the pressures under which we found ourselves. It became, in time, not a simple matter of going to the stars; it was a matter of pulling together a body of knowledge that might give us a clue to actions that might head off the Collapse foreseen by our social scientists. The common populace was not fully aware of the dangers seen by the scientists and they were generally not aware at all of what we were doing. For years they had been bombarded by warnings from all sorts of experts, most of whom were wrong, and they were so fed up with informed opinions that they paid no attention to anything that was being said. For they had no way of knowing which of them were sound.

"But there was this small group of scientists and engineers—and by a small group I mean some thousands of them—who saw the danger clearly. There might have been a number of ways in which the Collapse could have been averted, but the one that seemed to have the best chance was to gamble that from the knowledge that might be collected from those other civilizations among the stars, an answer might be found. It might, we told ourselves, be a basic answer we simply had not thought of, an answer entirely human in its concept, or it might be a completely alien answer which we could adapt."

He stopped and looked around the table. "Do you follow me?" he asked.

"I think we do," said Ezra. "You speak of ancient times that are unknown to us."

"But not to Mr. Cushing," said the A and R. "Mr. Cushing has read about those days."

"I cannot read," said Ezra. "There are very few who can. In all my tribe there is not a one who can."

"Which leads me to wonder," said the A and R, "how it comes about that Mr. Cushing can. You spoke of a university. Are there still universities?"

"Only one I know of," said Cushing. "There may be others,

but I do not know. At our university a man named Wilson, centuries ago, wrote a history of the Collapse. It is not a good history; it is largely based on legend."

"So you have some idea of what the Collapse was all about?"

"Only in a general way," said Cushing.

"But you knew about the Place of Going to the Stars?"

"Not from the history. Wilson knew of it, but he did not put it in his history. He dismissed it, I suppose, because it seemed too wild a tale. I found some of his notes, and he made mention of it in them."

"And you came hunting for it. But when you found it, you did not believe it could the place you were looking for. No launching pads, you said. At one time there were launching pads, quite some distance from this place. Then, after a time, after we saw that it wouldn't work, we asked ourselves if robotic probes would not work as well as men. . . ."

"The gossipers," said Cushing. "That is what they are— robotic interstellar probes. The Team looks on them as story tellers."

"The Team," said the A and R, "are a pair of busybodies from some very distant planet who intend some day to write what might be called 'The Decline and Fall of Technological Civilizations.' They have been vastly puzzled here, and I've made no attempt to set them straight. As a matter of fact, I've made it my business to further puzzle them. If I gave them any help, they would hang around for another hundred years, and I don't want that. I've had enough of them.

"The travelers—those probes you call the gossipers—could be made far more cheaply than starships. The research and development was costly, but once the design was perfected, with the various sensors all worked out, the information processing design—so that the probes could use their own data to work out information instead of just bringing back to us masses of raw data—once all this was done, they could be made much more cheaply than the ships. We built and programmed them by the hundreds and sent them out. In a century or so, they began coming back, each of them crammed with the information he'd collected and stored as code in his memory storage. There have been a few of them who have not come back. I suppose that accidents of various kinds might have happened to them. By the time the first of them started coming back, however, the Collapse had come about, and there were no humans left at this station. Myself and a few other robots, that was all. Now even the few other robots are gone. Through the years, there has been attrition: one of them killed in a rockfall; another falling victim to a strange disease—which puzzles me exceedingly, since such as we should be disease-immune. Another electrocuted in a moment of great carelessness, for despite the candle, we do have electricity. It is supplied by the solar panels that top this building. The candle is because we have run out of bulbs and there is no way to replace them. But, however that may be, in one way or another all the robots but myself became dysfunctional until only I was left.

"When the travelers came back, we transferred their coded data to the central storage facility in this place, reprogrammed them and sent them out again. In the course of the last few centuries I have not sent them out again as they came back. There has seemed little sense in doing so. Our storage banks are already crowded almost to capacity. As I transferred the data, I should, I suppose, have deactivated the travelers and stored them away, but it seemed a shame to do so. They do enjoy life so much. While the transfer to the central banks removes all the actual data, there is a residue of impressions remaining in the probes, only a shadow of the information that they carried, so that they retain a pseudomemory of what they have experienced and they spend their time telling one another of their great adventures. Some of them got away that first night you arrived, and before I called them back, they had given you a sample of their chatter. They do the same with the Team and I have made no attempt to stop them, for it gives the Team something to do and keeps those two roly-poly worthies off my back."

"So, laddie boy," said Meg to Cushing, "you have found your Place of Stars. Not the kind of place you looked for, but an even greater place."

"What I don't understand," said Cushing to the A and R, "is why you're talking to us. You sent us word—remember?—that the place was banned to us. What made you change your mind?"

"You must realize," said the A and R, "the need for security in a place as sensitive as this. When we began developing the facility, we looked for an insolated location. We planted the belt of Trees, which were genetically programmed to keep all intruders out, and planted around and outside the belt a ring of living rocks. The Trees were a passive defense; the rocks, if need be, active. Over the years, the rocks have been largely dispersed. Many of them have wandered off. The Trees were supposed to keep them in control, but in many cases this has not worked out. At the time this station was established, it seemed to be apparent that civilization was moving toward collapse, which meant not only that the station should be kept as secret as possible but that defenses be set up. Our hope was, of course, that collapse could be staved off for another few hundred years. If that had been possible, we might have been able to offer some assurance that we were working toward solutions. But we were given somewhat less than a hundred years. For a long time after the Collapse came about, we held our breath. By that time the Trees were well grown, but they probably would not have held against a determined attack made with flamethrowers or artillery. But our remote situation, plus the secrecy which had surrounded the project, saved us. The mobs that finally erupted to bring about the Collapse probably were too busy, even had they known of us, to take any notice of us. There were richer pickings elsewhere."

"But this doesn't explain what happened with our party," said Cushing. "Why did you change your mind?"

"I must explain to you a little further what has happened here," said the A and R. "After the human population finally died off, there were only robots left and, as I've told you, as the years went on, fewer and fewer of them. There was not much maintenance required, and so long as there were several of us left, we had no problem with it. You must realize that the data-storage system has been simplified as much as possible, so that there are no great intricacies that could get out of whack. But one system has got out of whack and presents some difficulties. For some reason that I am unable to discover, the retrieval system—"

"The retrieval system?"

"That part of the installation that enables the retrieval of data. There are mountains of data in there, but there is no way to get it out. In my humble and fumbling way I have tried to make some head or tail of it in hopes I could repair whatever might be wrong, but you must understand, I am no technician. My training is in administrative work. So we have the situation of having all that data and not being able to get at any of it. When you came along, I felt the faint flutter of some hope when the Trees reported to me that there were sensitives among you. I told the Trees to let you through. I had hopes that a sensitive might get at the data, might be able to retrieve it. And was shocked to find that your one outstanding sensitive was not looking at our data at all, but at something beyond our data, overlooking it as a thing of small consequence."

"But you said the Trees told you," protested Cushing. "It must be that you're a sensitive, yourself."

"A technological sensitivity," said the A and R. "I am so designed as to be keyed in to the Trees, but to nothing else. A sensitivity, of course, but a contrived and most selective one."

"So you thought that a human sensitive might get at the data. But when Elayne didn't do it—"

"I thought it was all a failure at the time," said the A and R, "but I've thought it over since, and now I know the answer. She is in no way a failure, but a sensitive that is too far reaching, too keyed in to universal factors, to be of any use to us. When she inadvertently caught a glimpse of what we have in the data storage, she was shocked at it, shocked at the chaos of it; for I must admit that it is chaos—billions of pieces of data all clumped into a pile. But then there came this morning another one of you. The one that you call Meg. She reached into the data; she touched it. She got nothing from it, but she was aware of it. . . ."

"Not until I had the brain case," said Meg. "It was the brain case that made it possible."

"I gave you the brain case as a crystal ball," said Rollo. "That was all it was. Just a shiny thing to help you concentrate."

"Rollo," said Meg. "Please forgive me, Rollo. It is more than that. I had hoped you would never have to know. Laddie boy and I knew, but we never told you."

"You're trying to tell us," said the A and R, "that the brain still lives within its case; that when a robotic body is inactivated or destroyed, the brain is unaffected, that it still lives on."

"But that can't be right," cried Rollo in a strangled voice. "It could not see or hear. It would be shut up inside itself. . . ."

"That is right," said Meg.

"For a thousand years," said Rollo. "For more than a thousand years."

Cushing said, "Rollo, we are sorry. That night long ago when you showed Meg the brain case—you remember, don't you?— she sensed then that the brain was still alive. She told me and we agreed that you should never know, that no one should ever know. You see, there was nothing anyone could do."

"There are millions of them," said Rollo. "Hidden away in places where they fell and will never be found. Others collected by the tribes and stacked in pyramids. Others used as childish playthings to roll along the ground. . . ."

"Being a robot, I mourn with you," said the A and R. "I am as shocked as you are. But I agree with the gentleman that there is nothing one can do."

"We could build new bodies," said Rollo. "At the least we could do something to give them back their sight and hearing. And their voices."

"Who would do all this?" asked Cushing bitterly. "A blacksmith at the forge of a farm commune? An ironworker who beats out arrowheads and spearpoints for a tribe of nomads?"

"And yet," said the A and R, "this present brain, isolated for all these years, was able to respond when it was touched by the probing of a human brain. Responded and was of help, I believe you said."

"I could see the spiders and the gnats," said Meg, "but they meant nothing to me. With the robot's brain, they became something else—a pattern, perhaps, a pattern in which there must have been a meaning, although I did not know the meaning."

"I think, however," said the A and R, "that herein lies some hope. You reached the data bank; you sensed the data; you were able to put them into visual form."

"I don't see how that helps too much," said Cushing. "Visual form is meaningless unless it can be interpreted."

"This was a beginning only," said the A and R. "A second time, a third time, a hundredth time, the meaning may become apparent. And this is even more likely if we should be able to muster, say, a hundred sensitives, each tied in with a robotic brain that might be able to reinforce the sensitive, as this robotic brain was able to make Meg see more clearly."

"This is all fine," said Cushing, "but we can't be sure that it will work. If we could repair the retrieval system . . ."

"I'll use your words," said the A and R. "Who'd do it? Blacksmiths and metalworkers? And even if we could repair it, how could we be sure that we could read the data and interpret it. It seems to me a sensitive would have a better chance of understanding what's packed away in there. . . ."

"Given time," said Cushing, "we might find men who could figure out a way to repair the retrieval. If they had diagrams and specs."

"In this place," said the A and R, "we have the diagrams and specs. I have pored over them, but to me they have no significance. I can make nothing of them. You say that you can read?"

Cushing nodded. "There's a library back at the university. But that would be of little help. It underwent an editing process, purged of everything that had been written some centuries before the Time of Trouble."

"We have a library here," said the A and R, "that escaped the editing. Here there'd be materials which might help to train the men you say might repair the system."

Ezra spoke up. "I've been trying to follow this discussion and am having trouble with it. But it appears there are two ways to go about it: either repair the retrieval system, or use sensitives. I'm a sensitive and so is my granddaughter, but I fear neither one of us could be of any help. Our sensitivities, it appears, are specialized. She is attuned to universalities, whereas I am attuned to plants. I fear this would be the case if we sought out sensitives. There are, I would suspect, very many different kinds of them."

"That is true," said Cushing. "Wilson had a chapter in his history that dealt with the rise of sensitives after the Collapse. He felt that technology had served as a repressive factor against the development of sensitives and that once the pressure of technology was removed, there were many more of them."

"This may be true," said Ezra, "but out of all of them, I would guess you could find very few who could do what Meg has done."

"We are forgetting one thing," said Meg, "and that is the robotic brain. I'm not so sure that my powers were so much reinforced by the brain. I would suspect I did no more than direct the brain into the data banks, making it aware of them, giving it a chance to see what was there and then tell me what was there."

"Sorrowful as the subject is to me," said Rollo, "I think that Meg is right. It's not the human sensitives but the brains that will give us answers. They have been shut up within themselves for all these centuries. In the loneliness of their situations, they would have kept on functioning. Given no external stimuli, they were forced back upon themselves. Since they had been manufactured to think, they would have thought. They would have performed the function for which they were created. They would have posed problems for themselves and tried to work through the problems. All these years they have been developing certain lines of logic, each one of them peculiar to himself. Here we have sharpened intellects, eager intellects. . . ."

"I subscribe to that," said Ezra. "This makes sense to me. All we need are sensitives who can work with the brains, serve as interpreters for the brains."

"Okay, then," said Cushing. "We need brains and sensitives. But I think, as well, we should seek people who might train themselves to repair the retrieval system. There is a library here, you say?"

"A rather comprehensive scientific and technological library," said the A and R. "But to use it, we need people who can read."

"Back at the university," said Cushing, "there are hundreds who can read."

"You think," said the A and R, "that we should attack our problem on two levels?"

"Yes, I do," said Cushing.

"And so do I," said Ezra.

"If we should succeed," said Cushing, "what would you guess we'd get? A new basis for a new human civilization? Something that would lift us out of the barbarism and still not set us once again on the old track of technology? I do not like the fact that we may be forced, through the necessity of repairing the retrieval system if the sensitive plan should fail, to go back to technology again to accomplish what we need."

"No one can be certain what we'll find," said the A and R. "But we would be trying. We'd not just be standing here."

"You must have some idea," Cushing insisted. "You must have talked to at least some of the returning probes, perhaps all of them, before transferring the data that they carried into the storage banks."

"Most of them," said the A and R, "but my knowledge is only superficial. Only the barest indication of what might be in the storage. Some of it, of course, is of but small significance. The probes, you must understand, were programmed only to visit those planets where there was a possibility life might have risen. If their sensors did not show indication of life, they wasted no time on a planet. But even so, on many of the planets where life had risen, there was not always intelligence or an analogue of intelligence. Which is not to say that even from such planets we would not discover things of worth."

"But on certain planets there was intelligence?"

"That is so," said the A and R. "On more planets than we had any reason to suspect. In many instances it was a bizarre intelligence. In some cases, a frightening intelligence. Some five hundred light years from us, for instance, we know of something that you might describe as a galactic headquarters, although that is a human and therefore an imprecise interpretation of what it really is. And even more frightening, a planet, perhaps a little shorter distance out in space, where dwells a race advanced so far beyond the human race in its culture that we would view its representatives as gods. In that race, it seems to me, is a real danger to the human race, for you always have been susceptible to gods."

"But you think there are some factors, perhaps many factors, from which we could choose, that would help to put we humans back on track again?"

"I'm positive," said the A and R, "that we'll find something if we have the sense to use it. As I tell you, I got just a faint impression of what the travelers carried. Just a glimpse of it, and perhaps not a glimpse of the important part of it. Let me tell you some of the things I glimpsed: a good-luck mechanism, a method whereby good luck could be induced or engineered; a dying place of a great confederation of aliens, who went there to end their days and, before they died, checked all their mental and emotional baggage in a place where it could be retrieved if there were ever need of it; an equation that made no sense to me, but that I am convinced is the key to faster-than-light travel; an intelligence that had learned to live parasitically elsewhere than in brain tissue; a mathematics that had much in common with mysticism and which, in fact, makes use of mysticism; a race that had soul perception rather than mere intellectual perception. Perhaps we could find use for none of these, but perhaps we could. It is a sample only. There is much more, and though much would be useless, I can't help but believe we'd find many principles or notions that we could adapt and usefully employ."

Elayne spoke for the first time. "We pluck only at the edge of it," she said. "We see all imperfectly. We clutch at small particulars and fail to comprehend the whole. There are greater things than we can ever dream. We see only those small segments that we can understand, ignoring and glossing over what we are not equipped to understand."

She was not talking to them but to herself. Her hands were folded on the tabletop in front of her and she was staring out beyond the walls that hemmed them in, staring out into that other world which only she could see.

She was looking at the universe.

24

"You're mad," Meg told Cushing. "If you go out to face them, they will gobble you. They're sore about our being here. Angry about our being here. . . ."

"They are men," said Cushing. "Barbarians. Nomads. But still they are men. I can talk with them. They are basically reasonable. We need brain cases; we need sensitives; we need men who have a technological sense. A native technologic sense. In the old days there were people who could look at something and know how it worked, instinctively know how it worked—able, almost at a glance, to trace out the relationship of its working parts."

"People in the old days," said Rollo, "but not now. Those people you talk about lived at a time when machines were commonplace. They lived with machines and by machines and they thought machines. And another thing: what we are talking about here is not crude machines, with interlocking gears and sprockets. The retrieval system is electronic and the electronic art was lost long ago. A special knowledge, years of training were required. . . ."

"Perhaps so," Cushing agreed, "but here the A and R has a tech library; at the university we have men and women who can read and write and who have not lost entirely the capacity and discipline for study. It might take a long time. It might take several lifetimes. But since the Collapse we have wasted a number of lifetimes. We can afford to spend a few more of them. What we must do is establish an elite corps of sensitives, of brain cases, of potential technologists, of academics. . . ."

"The brain cases are the key," said Meg. "They are our only hope. If there are any who have kept alive the old tradition of logic, they are the ones. With the help and direction of sensitives, they can reach the data and probably are the only ones who can interpret it and understand it once it's interpreted."

"Once they reach and explain it," said Cushing, "there must be those who can write it down. We must collect and record a body of data. Without that, without the meticulous recording of it, nothing can be done."

"I agree," said Rollo, "that the robotic brains are our only hope. Since the Collapse there has not been one iota of technological development from the human race. With all the fighting and raiding and general hell-raising that is going on, you would think that someone would have reinvented gunpowder. Any petty cheiftain would give a good right arm for it. But no one has reinvented it. So far as I know, no one has even thought to do so. You hear no talk of it. I tell you, technology is dead. Nothing can be done to revive it. Deep down in the fiber of the race, it has been rejected. It was tried once and failed, and that is the end of it. Sensitives and brain cases—those are what we need."

"The A and R indicated there are brain cases here," said Ezra. "The robots died, he's the only one that's left."

"A half dozen cases or so," said Meg. "We may need hundreds. Brain cases would not be the same. They'd be, I would guess, highly individualistic. Out of a hundred, you might find only one or two who could untangle what is to be found in the data banks."

"All right, then," said Cushing. "Agreed. We need a corps of sensitives; we need brain cases by the bagfull. To get them, we have to go to the tribes. Each tribe may have some sensitives; many of them have a hoard of cases. Some of the tribes are out there on the plain, just beyond the Trees. We don't have to travel far to reach them. I'll go out in the morning."

"Not you," said Rollo. "We."

"You'll stay here," said Cushing. "Once they caught sight of you, they'd run you down like a rabbit and have your brain case out. . . ."

"I can't let you go alone," protested Rollo. "We traveled all those miles together. You stood with me against the bear. We are friends, whether you know it or not. I can't let you go alone."

"Not just the one of you or the two of you," said Meg. "If one goes, so do all the rest of us. We're in this together."

"No, dammit!" yelled Cushing. "I'm the one to go. The rest of you stay here. I've told Rollo it's too dangerous for him. There is some danger for me, as well, I would imagine, but I think I can handle it. The rest of you we can't risk. You are sensitives and we need sensitives. They may be hard to find. We need all that we can find."

"You forget," said Ezra, "that neither Elayne nor I are the kind of sensitives you need. I can only talk with plants, and Elayne—"

"How do you know you can only talk with plants? You wanted it that way and that is all you've done. Even if it's all you can do, you can talk with the Trees and it may be important that we have someone who can talk with them. As for Elayne, she has an overall—a universal—ability that may stand us in good stead when we begin digging out the data. She might be able to see relationships that we couldn't see."

"But our own tribe may be out there," insisted Ezra. "If they are, it would help to have us along."

"We can't take the chance," said Cushing. "You can talk with your tribe for us later on."

"Laddie buck," said Meg, "mad I think you are."

"This is the kind of business," said Cushing, "that may call for a little madness."

"How can you be sure the Trees will let you out?"

"I'll talk with the A and R. He can fix it up for me."

25

Seen from close range, more of the nomads were camped on the prairie than Cushing had thought. The tepees, conical tents adapted from those used by the aboriginal North American plains tribes, covered a large area, gleaming whitely in the morning sun. Here and there across the level land were grazing horse bands, each of them under the watchful eyes of half a dozen riders. Trickles of smoke rose from fires within the encampment. Other than the horse herders and their charges, there was little sign of life.

The sun, halfway up the eastern sky, beat down mercilessly upon the prairie. The air was calm and muggy, bearing down so heavily that it required an effort to breathe.

Cushing stood just outside the Trees, looking the situation over, trying to calm the flutter of apprehension that threatend to tie his stomach into knots. Now that he was actually here, ready to begin his trudge across the naked land to the camp, he realized for the first time that there could be danger. He had said so when he had talked about it the previous afternoon, but it was one thing to think about it intellectually and another to be brought face to face with its possibility.

But the men out there, he told himself, would be reasonable. Once he had explained the situation, they would listen to him. Savages they might be, having turned to barbarism after the Collapse, but they still had behind them centuries of civilized logic that even a long string of generations could not have completely extinguished.

He set out, hurrying at first, then settling down to a more reasonable and less exhausting pace. The camp was some distance off and it would take a while to get there. He did not look back, but kept tramping steadily forward. Halfway there, he paused to rest and then turned to look back at the butte. As he turned, he saw the flash of the sun off a glittering surface well clear of the Trees.

Rollo, the damned fool, tagging along behind him!

Cushing waved his arms and shouted. "Go back, you fool! Go back!"

Rollo hesitated, then began to come on again.

"Go back!" yelled Cushing. "Get out of here. Vamoose. I told you not to come."

Rollo came to a stop, half lifted an arm in greeting.

Cushing made shoving motions at him.

Slowly Rollo turned, heading back toward the Trees. After a few steps, he stopped and turned. Cushing was still standing there, waving at him to go back.

He turned again and went plodding back the way he'd come. He did not turn again.

Cushing stood and watched him go. The sun still burned down, and far in the west a blackness loomed above the horizon. A storm, he wondered? Could be, he told himself; the very air smelled of heavy weather.

Convinced that Rollo would not follow him, he proceeded toward the camp. Now there was evidence of life. Dogs were sallying out from the fringes of the tepees, barking. A small band of horsemen were moving toward him at a walk. A gang of boys came out to the edge of the camp and hooted at him, the hoots small and tinny in the distance.

He did not break his stride. The horsemen came on at their steady gait.

They came up and halted, facing him. He said, gravely, "Good morning, gentlemen."

They did not respond, regarding him with stony faces. The line parted in the middle to let him through and, when he resumed his march, fell back to flank him on either side.

It was not good, he knew, but he must act as if it were. There could be no sign of fright. Rather, he must pretend that this was a signal honor, the sending out of an escort to conduct him into camp.

He strode along, not hurrying, eyes straight ahead, paying no attention to those who paced on either side of him. He felt sweat popping out of his armpits and trickling down his ribs. He wanted to wipe his face, but with an iron will refrained from doing so.

The camp was directly ahead and he saw that it was laid out with wide spaces serving as streets between the lines of tepees. Women and children stood before many of the tepees, their faces as stony as those of the men who moved beside him. Bands of small boys went whooping up and down the street.

Most of the women were hags. They wore misshapen woolen dresses. Their hair hung raggedly and was matted and dirty, their faces seamed and leathered from the sun and wind. Most of them were barefoot and their hands were gnarled with work. Some of them opened toothless mouths to cackle at him. The others were stolid, but wore a sense of disapproval.

At the far end of the street stood a group of men, all facing in his direction. As he came up the street, one of them moved forward with a shuffle and a limp. He was old and stooped. He wore leather breeches and a cougar hide was tossed across one shoulder, fastened with thongs in front. His snow-white hair hung down to his shoulders. It looked as if it had been cut off square with a dull knife.

A few feet from him Cushing stopped. The old man looked at him out of ice-blue eyes.

"This way," he said. "Follow me."

He turned and shuffled up the street. Cushing slowed his pace to follow.

To him came the smell of cooking, laced by the stink of garbage that had been too long in the summer heat. At the doorways of some of the lodges stood picketed horses, perhaps the prize hunters or war horses of their owners. Dogs, slinking about, emitted yelps of terror when someone hurled a stick at them. The heat of the sun was oppressive, making warm the very dust that overlay the street. Over all of this rode the sense of approaching storm—the smell, the feel, the pressure, of brewing weather.

When the old man came up to the group of men, they parted to let him through, Cushing following. The mounted escort dropped away. Cushing did not look to either side to glimpse the faces of the men, but he knew that if he had looked, he would have seen the same hardness that had been on the faces of the horsemen.

They broke through the ranks of men and came into a circle, rimmed by the waiting men. Across the circle a man sat in a heavy chair over which a buffalo robe was thrown. The old man who had served as Cushing's guide moved off to one side and Cushing walked forward until he faced the man in the chair.

"I am Mad Wolf," said the man, and having said that, said no more. Apparently he felt that anyone should know who he was once he had said his name.

He was a huge man, but not a brute. There was in his face a disquieting intelligence. He wore a thick black beard and his head was shaven. A vest of wolf skin, decorated by the tails of wolves, was open at the front, displaying a bronzed and heavily muscled torso. Hamlike hands grasped the chair arms on either side.

"My name is Thomas Cushing," Cushing told him.

With a shock, Cushing saw that the scarecrow man who had been spokesman for the wardens stood beside the chair.

"You came from Thunder Butte," rumbled Mad Wolf. "You are one of the party that used your magic tricks to get through the Trees. You have disturbed the Sleepers."

"There are no Sleepers to disturb," said Cushing. "Thunder Butte is the Place of Going to the Stars. There lies hope for the human race. I have come to ask for help."

"How for help?"

"We need your sensitives."

"Sensitives? Talk plainly, man. Tell me what you mean."

"Your witches and warlocks. Your medicine men, if you have such. People who can talk with trees, who bring the buffalo, who can divine the weather. Those who throw carven bones to see into the future."

Mad Wolf grunted. "And what would you do with those? We have very few of them. Why should we give the ones we have to you, who have disturbed the Sleepers?"

"I tell you there are no Sleepers. There were never any Sleepers."

The warden spoke. "There was one other among them who told us this same thing. A tall woman with emptiness in her eyes and a terrible face. 'You are wrong,' she told us, 'there aren't any Sleepers.'"

"Where is this woman now," Mad Wolf asked of Cushing, "with her empty eyes and her terrible face?"

"She stayed behind," said Cushing. "She is on the butte."

"Waking the Sleepers. . . ."

"Goddammit, don't you understand? I've told you, there are no Sleepers."

"There was with you, as well, a man of metal, one once called a robot, a very ancient term that is seldom spoken now."

"It was the metal man," the warden said, "who killed the bear. This one who stands before us shot arrows, but it was the metal man who killed the bear, driving a lance into the chest."

"That is true," said Cushing. "My arrows did but little."

"So you admit," said Mad Wolf, "that there is a metal man."

"That is true. He may be the last one left and he is a friend of mine."

"A friend?"

Cushing nodded.

"Are you not aware," asked Mad Wolf, "that a robot, if such it be, is an evil thing—a survival from that day when the world was held in thrall by monstrous machines? That it's against the law to harbor such a machine, let alone be a friend of one?"

"It wasn't that way," said Cushing. "Back there, before the Collapse, I mean. The machines didn't use us; we used the machines. We tied our lives to them. The fault was ours, not theirs."

"You place yourself against the legends of the past?"

"I do," said Cushing, "because I have read the History."

Perhaps, he thought, it was not wise to argue so with this man sitting in the chair, to contradict so directly all that he had said. But it would be worse, he sensed, to buckle in to him. It would not do to show a weakness. There still might be reason here. Mad Wolf still might be willing, once the initial sparring had been done, to listen to the truth.

"The History?" asked Mad Wolf, speaking far too softly. "What is this history that you speak of?"

"A history written by a man named Wilson, a thousand years ago. It's at a university. . . ."

"The university on the bank of the Mississippi? That is where you came from—a sniveling, cowardly egghead hoeing his potato patch and huddling behind a wall? You come walking in here, as if you had a right, wanting what you call our sensitives. . . ."

"And that's not all," said Cushing, forcing himself to speak as brashly as he could. "I want your blacksmiths and your spear- and arrow-makers. And I want the brain cases that you have."

"Ah, so," said Mad Wolf, still speaking softly. "This is all you want. You're sure there's nothing else?"

There was a secret amusement, a sly amusement, on the faces of the men who circled them. These men know their chief, knew the ways of him.

"That is all I'll need," said Cushing. "Given these things, it will be possible to find a better way of life."

"What is wrong with the way we live?" asked Mad Wolf. "What is bad about it? We have food to fill our bellies; we have far lands to roam in. We do not have to work. It is told that in the old days all men had to work. They woke and ate their breakfasts so they could get to work. They labored all the day and then went home again and tumbled early into bed so they could get up early to return to work. They had no time to call their own. For all this, they were no better off than we are. For all their labor, they got only food and sleep. This we get, and much more, and do not have to work for it. You have come from that egghead fort of yours to change all this, to go back to the olden ways, where we will labor dawn to dusk, working out our guts. You would wake the Sleepers, an event we have stationed guards all these centuries to guard against, so they cannot come ravening from the butte. . . ."

"I have told you there are no Sleepers," Cushing said. "Can't you take my word for that? Up there on the butte is knowledge that men have gathered from the stars. Knowledge that will help us, not to regain the old days, which were bad, but to find a new way."

It was no use, he knew. They did not believe him. He had been mistaken. There was no reason here. They would never believe him.

"The man is mad," the warden said.

"Yes, he truly is," said Mad Wolf. "We have wasted time on him."

Someone who had come up behind him seized Cushing, almost gently, but when he lunged to get away, hard hands closed upon him, forced his arms behind him and held him helpless.

"You have sinned," Mad Wolf told him. "You have sinned most grievously." To the men who had their hands on Cushing, he said, "Tie him to the post."

The men who had stood in the circle now were breaking up, wandering away, and as they left, Cushing saw the post which until now had been hidden by their massed bodies. It stood no more than five feet high, fashioned from a new-cut tree, perhaps a cottonwood, with the bark peeled from it.

Without a word the men who held him forced him to the post, pulled his arms behind the post and tied them there, the thongs positioned in deep notches on either side of the post so he could not slide them free. Then, still without a word, they walked away.

He was not alone, however, for the gangs of small boys still were on the prowl.

He saw that he was in what appeared to be the center of the

encampment. The larger space where the post was planted was the hub of a number of streets that ran between the lodges.

A clod of dirt went humming past his head, another hit him in the chest. The gang of boys ran down the street, howling at their bravado.

For the first time, Cushing noticed that the sun had gone and the landscape darkened. An unnatural silence encompassed everything. A great black cloud, almost purple in its darkness, boiled out of the west. The first broken forerunners of the cloud, racing eastward, had covered the sun. Thunder rumbled far off, and above the butte a great bolt of lightning lanced across the heavy blackness of the cloud.

Somewhere in one of the lodges, he told himself, the principal men of the tribe, among them Mad Wolf and the warden, were deciding what was to be done with him. He had no illusions, no matter the form their decision took, what the end result would be. He pulled against the thongs, testing them. They were tight; there was no give in them.

It had been insane, of course, this gamble of his—that men still might listen to reason. He realized, with a faint, ironic amusement, that he'd not been given a chance to explain what it was all about. His conversation with Mad Wolf had been in generalities. The failure of his attempt, he knew, hung on the concept of the Sleepers, a myth repeated so many times over so long a time that it had taken on the guise of gospel. Yet, yesterday, when he had talked it over with the others, he had been convinced that if his arguments were properly presented, there was better than an even chance they would be listened to. It was his years at the university, he told himself, that had betrayed him. A man who dwelled in a place of sanity was ill-equipped to deal with reality, a reality that still was colored by Collapse fanaticism.

He wondered, with a quaint sense of unreality, what would

happen now. None of those still on the butte was equipped to carry forward the work, even to attempt to begin to form the organization of an elite corps that over the years could wrest the secrets from the data banks. Rollo was canceled out; as a robot he had no chance at all. Through Meg, for all her ability, ran a streak of timidity that would make her helpless. Ezra and Elayne were simply ineffectual.

Andy, he thought, half-grinning to himself. If Andy could only talk, he would be the best bet of them all.

Heavy peals of thunder were rippling in the west, and above the crest of Thunder Butte the lightning ran like a nest of nervous snakes. Heat and mugginess clamped down hard against the land. The huge cloud of purple blackness kept on boiling higher into the sky.

People were coming out of the lodges now—women and children and a few men. The hooting boys threw more clods and stones at him, but their aims were poor. One small pebble, however, hit him on the jaw and left a paralyzing numbness. Down the street he could see, still far out on the prairie, the guards driving a herd of horses toward the camp.

Watching the horses, he saw them break into a run, thundering toward the camp, with the guards frantically quirting their mounts in an endeavor to head them off or slow them down. Something had spooked the herd—that was quite evident. A sizzling lightning bolt, perhaps, or a nearby crack of thunder.

At the far edge of the camp someone shouted in alarm and the shout was picked up by others, the frightened shouts ringing through the camp between the pealing of the thunder. People were piling in panic out of the lodges, filling the street, running and screaming, instinctively reacting to the terror of the shouting.

Then he saw it, far off—the flicker of the lights, the zany sparkle of many Shivering Snakes against the blackness of the sky, riding before the approaching storm, sweeping toward the camp. He caught his breath and strained against the thongs. The Snakes, he asked himself, what were those crazy Snakes about?

But it was not, he saw, as the Snakes swept closer, the Snakes alone. Andy ran at the head of them, mane and tail flowing in the wind, his feet blurred with the speed of his running, while beside him raced the pale glimmer that was Rollo, and behind them and to each side of them, the dark blobs of a great horde of Followers, seen in the darkness only by virtue of the Snakes that spun in dizzy circles about each of them, illuminating them, picking out the wolflike shape of them. And behind the pack, the bouncing, bobbing spheres that were the Team, straining to keep up.

At the edge of the camp the frightened horse herd came plunging down the street, rearing madly, screaming in their terror, careening into lodges that came tumbling down. People were running madly and without seeming purpose, screaming mouths open like wide *O*'s in the center of their faces. Not only women and children but men as well, running as if the hounds of hell were snapping at their heels.

As the horses came at him, Cushing hunkered low against the post. A lashing hoof grazed a shoulder as a screaming horse reared and swerved to go around him. Another crashed into a lodge and fell, bringing the lodge down with him, collapsed, tangled amid the leather and the poles, kicking and striking with its forefeet in an effort to get free. Out from under the fallen lodge crawled a man, clawing to pull himself along until he was able to get on his legs and run. A lightning flash, for a moment, lined his face, lighting it so it could be recognized. It was Mad Wolf.

Then Rollo was beside Cushing, knife in hand, slashing at the thongs. The camp was deserted now except for a few people still trapped beneath the fallen lodges, howling like gut-shot dogs as they fought their way to freedom. All about, the Shivering Snakes swirled in loops of fire and the Followers were dancing, with Andy capering in their midst.

Rollo put his head down close to Cushing's ear and shouted so he could hear above the steady roll of thunder. "This should take care of it," he shouted. He swept an arm at the camp. "We don't need to worry about them anymore. They won't stop running until they are over the Missouri."

Beside Rollo bounced one of the Team, jittering in excitement. It bellowed at Cushing, "Fun you say we do not have and we know not what you speak of. But now we know. Rollo say to come and see the fun."

Cushing tried to answer Rollo, but his words were swept away and drowned as the forefront of the storm crashed down upon them in a howl of rushing wind and a sudden sheet of water that beat like a hammer on the ground.

26

The dry cactus plains of the Missouri were behind them and ahead lay the rolling home prairies of the one-time state of Minnesota. This time, Cushing reminded himself, with some satisfaction, they need not follow the winding, time-consuming course of the gentle Minnesota River, but could strike straight across the prairie for the ruined Twin Cities of Minneapolis and St. Paul and their final destination, the university. No nomad band, no city tribe, would even think of interfering with their march.

The first frosts of autumn had touched the trees with brushes of gold and red; hardy prairie flowers bloomed on every side. When spring came around, they would head back again for Thunder Butte, this time with a string of packhorses carrying supplies and with at least a few university residents added to the expedition. Perhaps, he thought, with more than that—some sensitives, perhaps, and a few brain cases, for during the winter, they would contact some of the city tribes and more eastern bands, who might be more open to reason than the nomad encampment had proved to be.

Far ahead of them Rollo ranged, scouting out the land, and, at a shorter distance, Andy, with his pack of Followers gamboling all about him like a bunch of pups at play. The Team rolled along sedately to one side, and, sparkling in the pleasant autumn sunshine, the swarms of Shivering Snakes were everywhere. They accompanied Rollo on his scouting runs; they danced with the Followers and with Andy; they swung in shimmering circles about everyone.

"You'll clean me out," the A and R had said in mock sorrow when they left. "You'll leave me not a single Follower or Snake. It's that silly horse of yours and that equally silly robot. They, the two of them, blot up all the crazy things they meet. Although, I'm glad they're going, for any roving band that might intend to do you dirt will reconsider swiftly when they see the escort that goes along with you."

"We'll head back," promised Cushing, "as soon as winter lifts enough to travel. We'll waste no time. And I hope we'll have others with us."

"I've been alone so long," the A and R had said, "that such a little interval does not really matter. I can wait quite easily, for now I have some hope."

Cushing cautioned him, "You must realize that it all may come to nothing. Try as hard and earnestly as we may, we may not be able to untangle the mysteries of the data. Even if we do, we may find nothing we can use."

"All that man has done throughout his history," said the A and R, "has been a calculated gamble without assurance of success. The odds, I know, are long, but in all honesty, we can ask for nothing better."

"If Mad Wolf had only gone along with us. If he had only listened."

"There are certain segments of society that will never lend an ear to a new idea. They squat in a certain place and will not budge from it. They will find many reasons to maintain a way of life that is comfortable to them. They'll cling to old religions; they'll fasten with the grip of death on ethics that were dead, without their knowing it, centuries before; they will embrace a logic that can be blown over with a breath, still claiming it is sacrosanct.

"But I'm not like this. I am a foolish sentimentalist and my optimism is incurable. To prove that, I shall start, as soon as you are gone, sending out the probes again. When they begin returning, a hundred years from now, a millennium from now, we shall be here and waiting, eager to find out what they have brought back, hoping it will be something we can use."

At times there had been small bands of scouts who sat their horses on a distant skyline and looked them over, then had disappeared, carrying back their word to the waiting tribes. Making sure, perhaps, that the march of this defiant group still traveled under the protection of the grotesques from Thunder Butte.

The weather had been good and the travel easy. Now that they had reached the home prairies, Cushing estimated that in another ten days they'd be standing before the walls of the university. There they would be accepted. There they would find those who would listen and understand. It might be, he thought, that it was for that very moment that the university had preserved itself all these long years, keeping intact a nucleus of sanity that would be open to a new idea—not accepting it blindly, but for study and consideration. When they set out next spring for Thunder Butte, there would be some from the university, he was certain, who would travel the return journey with them.

Meg was a short distance ahead of him and he trotted to

catch up with her. She still carried the brain case, awkward as it might be to carry. During all the miles they'd traveled, it had been always with her. She had clutched it to her, even in her sleep.

"One thing we must be sure of," she had told him days before. "Any sensitive who uses a brain case must realize and accept the commitment to it. Once having made contact with it, that contact must continue. You cannot awaken a brain, then walk away from it. It becomes, in a way, a part of you. It becomes best friend, your other self."

"And when a sensitive dies?" he asked. "The brain case can outlive many humans. When the best friend human dies, what then?"

"We'll have to work that out," she said. "Another sensitive standing by, perhaps, to take over when the first one's gone. Another to replace you. Or, by that time, we may have been able to devise some sort of electronic system that can give the brain cases access to the world. Give them sight and hearing and a voice. I know that would be a return to technology, which we have foresworn, but, laddie boy, it may be we'll have to make certain accommodations to technology."

That might be true, he knew—if they only could. Thinking of it, he was not sure that it was possible. Many years of devoted research and development lay as a background to the achievement of even the simplest electronic device. Even with the technological library at the Place of Going to the Stars, it might not be possible to pick up the art again. For it was not a matter of the knowledge only, of knowing how it worked. It was, as well, the matter of manufacturing the materials that would be needed. Electronics had been based not on the knowledge of the art alone but on a massive technological capability. Even in his most hopeful moments he was forced to realize that it was probably now beyond man's capacity to reproduce a system that would replace that old lost capability.

In destroying his technologic civilization, man might have made an irreversible decision. In all likelihood, there was no going back. Fear alone might be a deterrent, the deep, implanted fear that being successful, there'd be no stopping place; that once reinstituted, technology would go on and on, building up again the monster that had once been killed. It was unlikely that such a situation could come about again, and so the fear would not be valid, but the fear would still be there. It would inhibit any move to regain even a part of what had been lost in the Time of Trouble.

So, if mankind were to continue in other than the present barbarism, a new path must be found, a new civilization based on some other method than technology. In sleepless nights he had tried to imagine that other method, that other path, and there had been no way to know. It was beyond his mental capability to imagine. The primordial ancestor who had chipped a rock to fashion the first crude tool could not have dreamed of the kind of tools that his descendants would bring about, based on the concept implicit in the first stone with a contrived cutting edge. And so it was in the present day. Already mankind, unnoticed, might have made that first faltering step toward the path that it would follow. If it had not, the answer, or many different answers, might be in the data banks of Thunder Butte.

He caught up with Meg and walked beside her.

"There is one thing, laddie boy, that worries me," she said. "You say the university will let us in and accept us and I have no doubt of that, for you know the people there. But what about the Team? Will they accept the Team? How will they relate to them?"

Cushing laughed, realizing it was the first time he had laughed in days.

"That will be beautiful," he said. "Wait until you see it. The Team picking the university apart, the university picking the Team apart. Each of them finding out what makes the other tick."

He threw up his head and laughed again, his laughter rolling across the plains.

"My God," he said, "it will be wonderful. I can't wait to see it."

Now he let the thought creep in—the thought that until now he had firmly suppressed in a reluctance to allow himself even to think of a hope that might not be there.

The Team was made up of two alien beings, living representatives of another life form that had achieved intelligence and that must have formed a complex civilization earmarked by an intellectual curiosity. Intellectual curiosity would be, almost by definition, a characteristic of any civilization, but a characteristic that might vary in its intensity. That the Team's civilization has more than its full share of it was evidenced by their being here.

It was just possible that the Team might be willing, perhaps even eager, to help mankind with its problems. Whether they could offer anything of value was, of course, unknown; but, lacking anything else of value, the alien direction of their thought processes and their viewpoints might provide new starting points for man's own thinking, might serve to short-circuit the rut in which man was apt to think, nudging him into fresh approaches and nonhuman logic.

In the free interchange of information and opinion that would take place between the Team and the university, much might be learned by both sides. For although the university no longer could qualify as an elite intellectual community, the old tradition of learning, perhaps even of research, still existed there. Within its walls were men and women who could still be stirred by that intellectual thirst which in ages past had shaped the culture mankind had built and then in a few months time had brought down to destruction.

Although not entirely to destruction, he reminded himself. On Thunder Butte the last remnants, the most sophisticated remnants, of that old, condemned technology still remained. Ironically, that remnant was now the one last hope of mankind.

What might have happened, he asked himself, if man had withheld his destruction of technology for a few more centuries? If he had, then the full force of it would have been available to work out the possible answers contained in the data banks of Thunder Butte. But this, he realized, might not necessarily have followed. The sheer weight, the arrogant power, of a full-scale, runaway technology might have simply rejected, overridden and destroyed what might be there as irrelevant. After all, with as great a technology as mankind possessed, what was the need of it?

Perhaps, just possibly, despite all man's present shortcomings, it might be better this way. As a matter of fact, we're not so badly off, he told himself. We have a few things on which to pin some hopes—Thunder Butte, the Team, the university, the still-living robotic brains, the unimpeded rise of sensitive abilities, the Trees, the Snakes, the Followers.

And how in the world could the Snakes or Followers—? And then he sternly stopped this line of thought. When it came to hope, you did not write off even the faintest hope of all. You held on to every hope; you cherished all; you let none get away.

"Laddie boy," said Meg. "I said it once before, and I'll say it now again. It's been a lovely trip."

"Yes," said Cushing. "Yes, you are right. It has been all of that."

More top science fiction available from Magnum Books

John Brunner

413 3458	The Wrong End of Time	55p
417 0208	Traveller in Black	75p

Philip K. Dick

413 3654	Dr Futurity	85p
413 3655	The Unteleported Man	80p
413 3653	The Crack in Space	70p
417 0197	The Simulacra	75p
477 0259	The Man Who Japed	85p

Damon Knight

417 0220	Off Centre	70p
417 0222	In Deep	75p
417 0221	Far Out	90p

Andrew J. Offutt

417 0190	Messenger of Zhuvastou	80p
417 0215	The Castle Keeps	85p
417 0302	The Clansman of Andor	90p

Clifford D. Simak

413 3690	Way Station	65p
417 0204	Cemetery World	70p
413 3695	Time Is The Simplest Thing	70p
413 3768	Time and Again	75p
417 0171	A Choice of Gods	70p
417 0236	So Bright the Vision	70p
417 0196	Shakespeare's Planet	75p

Olaf Stapledon

417 0274	Last And First Men	£1.25
417 0250	Last Men In London	£1.25

These and other Magnum Books are available at your bookshop or newsagent. In case of difficulties orders may be sent to:

Magnum Books
Cash Sales Department
P.O. Box 11
Falmouth
Cornwall TR10 109EN

Please send cheque or postal order, no currency, for purchase price quoted and allow the following for postage and packing:

U.K. 19p for the first book plus 9p per copy for each additional book ordered, to a maximum of 73p.

B.F.P.O. 19p for the first book plus 9p per copy for the next 6 books, thereafter 3p per & Eire book.

Overseas 20p for the first book and 10p per copy for each additional customers book.

While every effort is made to keep prices low, it is sometimes necessary to increase prices at short notice. Magnum books reserve the right to show new retail prices on covers which may differ from those previously advertised in the text or elsewhere.